WHIP it out

KAT ADDAMS

Visit my website at www.kataddams.com
Cover Designer: Lori Jackson, Lori Jackson Design,
lorijacksondesign.com
Editor and Interior Designer: Jovana Shirley,
Unforeseen Editing, www.unforeseenediting.com

This book is a work of fiction. Names, characters, places,
and incidents either are products of the author's
imagination or are used fictitiously. Any resemblance to
actual persons, living or dead, events, or locales is entirely
coincidental.

ISBN-13: 978-1-7331523-6-5

"Physical strength in a woman—that's what I am."

—Tina Turner

ONE

Betty

"This used to be my safe nest, and now, look at it." Rox shook her head. Her hands curled around an iron bar as she popped it into place.

"Yeah, it's still a safe nest. If you know the safe word." I held the other end of the bar and fumbled with the directions in my hand.

We had been putting my sex swing together for three hours, and we still couldn't get it right.

"Did you order this thing used or something? Is it missing parts? Can't we just call Jay?" She groaned, raking her fingers through a pile of screws and bolts.

"Damn it, Rox. We don't need a man. We're going to set up my playroom like the badass bitches we are. DTF. Dirty. Tough. Female. Has Jay got you forgetting who you are? We can do this. Now, hand me that long metal thing beside you."

"That's an Allen wrench, Miss Independent." Rox tossed the tool next to me and smiled. "He does have me goo-goo-eyed still, doesn't he?" She let out a long-drawn-out sigh.

"Keep that mess to yourself. You see, y'all have something special. But me? If I were to find a man like that, no good would come of it, I'm telling ya. All the women in my family have been divorced. Some more than once. You know that. It just doesn't work out for us Willis women like that. If I fell in love with a man like your Aussie next door, he would have a secret family still over there in the Down Under. I'd only find out about her and his babies after he died." I stuck the Allen wrench in a hole, as per the instructions, and began to tighten the legs on my new toy.

"Bullshit. You know your conniving ass would find out way before he died. That's why you got this room, isn't it? You tie these poor men up and make them tell you everything, so you can protect yourself when you move forward with them."

I set the wrench down and blinked. "Huh. I never thought about that. I always just thought I liked to dominate their asses. But that was some deep stuff you said. I take it, you're still in therapy."

"You know it."

"Proud of you. Even if you're peeling the layers of me back and exposing some shit I don't want to think about. So, cut it out. Let's just pretend that whip over there is for pleasure and not protection." I tilted my chin in the direction of a rack that held not one, or two, or three leather whips, but eight.

I had a whip of every size for a man of every size.

Tall and lanky?

Check!

Short and muscular?

Check!

Dad bod incoming?

Check!

I wasn't picky, but lately, I'd been leaning toward the stereotypical ripped-up men. Blame it on all of the male strippers I'd been eyeing at The Steamy Clam. Thanks to our ever-so-popular stripper friend Nikki, better known as Crystal Cream Pie, my taste in men had changed slightly. I never knew what a pair of pecs could do for me until I saw Terrance shake it onstage. Even after Nikki quit dancing, the girls and I would still stop by the club and have a good time.

"Let me get this straight. What you're saying is, we're putting up this sex swing, so you can finally invite Terrance over and torture him until he tells you all his secrets. Then, you can let yourself fall in love with him." Rox rose to her feet and snapped another iron bar into place.

A chill ran up my spine. Ever since Rox and Nikki had been messing with all those crystals and otherworldly stuff, I swore, sometimes, I thought they could read my mind, just like right now. I'd been thinking of Terrance, and Rox had sensed it.

"Can you get out of my head, please? Why don't you open up shop as a fortune-teller? You and Nikki. Take Layla too. I'll run The Pink Taco Truck, and y'all three can use your crystals and voodoo to fight crime or some shit. Get people laid. Go out into the world and do what you got to do to make it a better place." I pushed myself off the floor and reached for the other side of the swing, picking it up and joining it with the other half.

"I'm just saying, you've been eyeballing him for months. Y'all always flirt at Scarlett Herb when he's making your drinks. And then, when he dances, you're his number one fan. So, why haven't either of you asked the other out yet? Or at least fucked. One-night stand? Hello? What's wrong with you? The man is hot!" She pushed down hard on the roped seat of the swing, checking its sturdiness.

"You heard what Jay told us when we first started hanging around his bar. He said that Terrance has women in and out of there all the time. Some old ones, some young ones. He's into a little bit of everything. So, to me, it sounds like Terrance—aka stripper Tito—is a playboy. Why else would he be stripping? I'm sure he makes enough off all the tips he's pulling in. I know Jay pays his workers living wages. I'm not getting involved with Terrance or Tito or anyone who's going to put me on a list. One-night stand? Maybe. But I don't need all that right now. I'm working, paying bills, slaying goals." I sat my ass down in the swing and pushed through my heels, sending my body flying backward and my legs up to the ceiling.

"Good Lord. Is that what you're going to do in that thing? I might need to borrow it. Who's going to be the first to test it out anyway? If you say you aren't getting involved with a man, then what's all this for?" She motioned around my sex dungeon.

"I didn't say I don't have sex. I have friends with benefits. You know, the usual gang. I don't know yet who's going to get into this thing. Mike, Larry, Kenneth—"

"Tito."

"Girl, please. No time for a playboy."

"I see. So, only you're allowed to be the playboy in the relationship." She rubbed her chin. "You should still ask him out. Maybe he isn't a playboy. Or maybe he is, but he might change if he met the right person."

"Now, I know your ass needs to go back to therapy. You can't change a person!" I skidded to a stop.

"I'm not saying you can! I know you can't, believe me. You know I know that. But I'm saying if he saw something he wanted—like your tall, fine Black ass dressed in leather and holding a whip—then maybe, just maybe, he would cut all that riffraff out and be yours. I mean, most people stop looking once they meet the right one. It's not you changing anyone. It's just them not caring about anyone else once they see perfection." She walked over to the bed and let herself fall back on my new, bouncy mattress.

I detangled myself from the straps of my swing and followed her to the bed, plopping myself on my back beside her.

"I'm not anything close to perfection. No one is." I rubbed my palms over my tired eyes.

"No, we aren't perfect. But … you're wrong in saying you're not close. You're close to perfection for the right person."

"There you go with that la-la love-land shit you're in."

She propped herself up on her elbow, staring down into my face. "What is it you want then? You're thirty-one. Don't you want kids and a family? I know you do, Betty. Don't play tough with me."

"I have my nieces for family. What I want is, not to lose focus on my work and fall into poverty. I grew up that way, you know. Have you ever felt hunger, Rox? Do you know how many days I'd sometimes go without a meal? Ever gone to school for days on an empty stomach? I'd sneak to the back of the line, so I could pick food off trays when everyone set them on the counter to be thrown out. What if something happened and I couldn't provide for my children?"

"What in the hell are you talking about? You work with me. We own two taco trucks. We're both financially stable and independent. I know you are if I am. I know how much you make. We're a team. You just moved into my old house! Are you on crack? You've got it all. If you ever say you're going to wait until you're ready, you'll never get what you want. And I know you. Play tough all you want, but I know you. There's a heart somewhere in that cold, dead soul of yours. I know it because I hide mine too. That's why we're best friends."

"I thought we were best friends because we knew too much about each other." I rose on my elbow to meet her gaze.

"That too." She laughed.

"I do have it all." I glanced around my room.

Just a few short months ago, I had lived in an apartment that was crumbling before my eyes. Literally. When I banged my ex-boyfriend in there, anytime my headboard hit against the wall, dust would fall in our eyes from the old, retro ceiling. To make matters worse, it was one of those glittery ceilings. When we finished screwing, we'd both look like we'd stepped out of a dirty disco.

"Just not a man."

"Yep. And who says we need a man? Look at that. We just put that together all by ourselves." I nodded toward the swing, which made a squeaking noise, shifted, and collapsed on the ground.

"I rest my case," Rox muttered, hurling herself off the bed and walking toward her phone that she had placed on the dresser. "I'm calling Jay, and he'll bring some power tools. Then, we're finishing your sex dungeon within the next hour or two. While he's here, grill him about Terrance. Or I will. I see the way he looks at you and the way you look at him. Wouldn't hurt to try it out. Besides, what do you have to lose? You said it yourself. You have it all."

I bit my tongue. I couldn't argue with her on that. For once, I was happy and settled in life. If I added a man into the mix, that could all change. Given my family's track record on relationships, my entire life could be turned upside down by one douche bag. I rolled my eyes into the back of my head and lay down again.

"Fine. Call Jay. Let's get this damn thing together. But I'll be the one asking the Terrance questions."

"Good. And anything you don't find out, you can bring him over here and whip it out of him. Make that playboy pay for his naughty behavior! Show him who's boss!" She thrust her hips in the air and made a spanking motion with her palm before turning her attention to her phone.

I closed my eyes, drowning out the sounds of her conversation with her boyfriend, and focused on the next steps in my life. I'd not given any thought to it before. I'd learned from my childhood to live one day at a time. The only planning for the future I'd ever done was financial. But now, I was secure, and now, I had no idea what came next. I didn't need anything to come next, but I wasn't getting any younger. The thought of kids and family terrified me, but that tiny heart Rox had mentioned did ache for that so-called American dream one day. That day just wasn't going to be today or tomorrow or the next few years. I'd been saving every cent, and both kids and men could wipe out my cash quicker than I'd saved it—which had taken me years.

Nope, I'm not ready yet, I thought to myself. *I've got too much work to do, too much planning, saving for …*

I had no idea what I was saving for.

My future kids' college funds one day? Big house on ten acres? A vacation home in Greece?

"He'll be right over," Rox said, interrupting my thoughts.

It was a welcome interruption. These deep thoughts needed to go.

"You got one of the good ones, you know. You're lucky." I smiled, genuinely proud of my friend. I hadn't seen her this happy ever.

When Jay had walked into her life, Rox shone brighter than any of the DTF crew could imagine. I didn't want to get all crazy like Nikki and believe the hocus-pocus, but Jay and Rox were proof enough of how someone could walk into your life and change the course of your path forever.

"Thanks. I know. It's an amazing feeling. We're going to get your dark soul to feel it. You think you're doing good and have it all now? Wait until you meet *the one*." She sighed, letting herself free fall again onto my bed.

"Uh-huh. The one had better not fuck up what I have. I've worked too hard for it. I'm happy. Whoever he is, he'd better be perfect."

"Not perfect, but damn near it. I promise he will be. You just need to slow down and open your eyes. It's time. You deserve it." She rolled over and kissed the top of my forehead. "Just don't show him this room until much, much later into your relationship. I think those things might scare some men off." She nodded toward a shelf where dildos of all shapes and sizes were displayed.

"He's gonna like me for me. And this is me."

"True that," she agreed. "Just hide that spiked one at least. And maybe the dragon one you got from Weston's ma. Take it out once you've got him bound to this bed and talking but not before."

"Girl, I got this." I huffed on my nails and polished them against my chest.

TWO

Terrance

Betty had come into Scarlett Herb again the other night, making the Shizzle Sauce for our cocktails. I'd made her two drinks, in hopes she would loosen up enough to make a move, but she never did. I didn't know if she'd held back because we worked together on this restaurant collaboration or because I was a stripper man-whore. Whatever it was, we'd been flirty for months, and neither of us had taken it past that.

It wasn't that I needed sex or love or anything really. The only thing that could make me happier in life right now would be to retire early and live on an exotic beach. But that wouldn't happen. I had bills to pay, and stripping and bartending paid the bills. The tips I'd received from women were shocking at first. Sure, I knew women were just as horny as men. But I'd had no idea they were willing to pass out the big bucks for me to shake my sweaty johnson in their faces. No complaints here. It was easy money although tiring.

I groggily rinsed out the champagne flutes as I began to prep for Thirsty Thursday at the restaurant. Last night had been Wet Wednesday at The Steamy Clam, which meant I'd stayed there until two in the morning, making lonely women's panties soaked.

"Long night again?" my boss, Jay, asked, coming around the bar to help me.

"You can say that. Where's Aiden today?" I asked.

Jay's brother, Aiden, who was also my other boss, had been absent a lot lately. Their restaurant had taken off this year, and Aiden had been busy scouting new establishments to open our second location.

"Oh, you know, touring real estate. Haven't found much in Outer Forks yet though. We might end up building. That's just going to take a huge cut into our financials. Can't live life without risks. Sometimes, they pay off." Jay smiled, grabbing a dishrag and wiping down the bar.

"You can say that again," I mumbled. "Speaking of risks, what do you know about Betty? She's Rox's best friend, so you have to know some details. We flirt off and on but never past that. I think I want to take it to the next level and ask her out. There's just something about her bossy attitude that I like."

Jay's eyebrows creased. He set down his rag, scratching his head and letting out a long breath. "Betty, eh? Well, I know a fair bit about her. I know that she and Rox both come from hard times and that Betty likes to tell people she'll skin them alive if they ever bring trouble for either of them."

"Oh, yeah, I've gotten that from her plenty … and I like it."

"Do you now?" Jay smiled. His Australian accent always made me feel like I needed to go back to grammar school. My country twang couldn't keep up. "A bit of a masochist?" He prodded.

"Oh, who, me? No way," I said in my huskiest voice. "I wear the pants in all my relationships." I puffed up my chest and flexed my biceps while drying a wineglass.

"Too bad. Because I do know that—"

The front door to the restaurant flew open as Betty walked through, interrupting our conversation. Her hair trailed behind her as she stomped her heels over to the bar.

"I can't find my wallet. The last place I had it was here, Mr. Playboy. How am I going to stuff those ones down your pants when you're swiping my cash out from under me?" She put her hands on her hips and grinned.

"Hold on now! I wouldn't do anything like that! And I've not seen your wallet. I closed last night, and obviously, I'm opening today. Let me check the back, where we keep missing items. Maybe Aiden or one of the other mixologists picked it up."

"Mixologist? Well, isn't that a fancy word for bartender?" She rolled her eyes.

"Senior mixologist." I grinned before rushing off toward the storage room in the back.

My pulse quickened. The way Betty had stood there like she wanted to kill me sent a flush throughout my entire body. I closed my eyes for a split second and readjusted my hard-on, hiding it behind my apron as best as I could.

"What else you swiping? Old ladies' jewelry when they stick their hands down your G-string at the strip club?" Betty popped up behind me, sending me into a girlish scream.

"No." I cleared my throat and again gave my best burly voice. "I wouldn't do that! Man, do you have this bad impression of me or all men?" I picked up our lost-and-found box.

"All men. So far anyway. Now, give me that." She snatched the box from my hand and picked her leather wallet off the top, stuffing it into her purse. "Hmm. Thank you. Now, if you'll excuse me, I have some work to do." She turned on her heels to leave.

I stood, mesmerized, as her perfectly round ass bounced down the hallway. I loved every part of a woman, but I was through and through an ass man. One handful of that sweet butt cheek, and the animal in me awakened. I shook myself out of my trance. I'd had Betty alone for the first time, and I hadn't even made a move.

"Wait!" I called out after her, running to catch up. "You really believe all men are douche bags? Stealing your money even?"

"Of course, not all men! But I have run into some who have been spiking my drinks lately." She folded her arms across her chest and leaned back as if she was taking my whole being into view.

I wasn't sure what went through that feisty brain of hers, but the vicious smirk she wore on her face caused my cock to stir again.

"What do you mean? You order alcoholic beverages, and I heavy-hand it. It's like me giving you more than what you pay for, like a bonus. I thought you might like that. I don't do that for everyone, you know."

"Only all those women who are coming and going with you from what I hear. Are you Terrance the mixologist or your stripper name, Tito the Mixmaster? Just like a man to have an alter ego. Don't get me wrong. I like the wild demon you let out. But I also like authenticity. With you, I don't know what I'll get. It seems to me like you have a hectic and very exciting life. Taking home women left and right."

"Huh?" I gulped. I knew exactly what she was talking about. "That's not what it looks like. I'm not a playboy." Lie number one. Kind of.

I wasn't a playboy anymore. I had been, but I had turned a new leaf just two months ago. I had decided it was time for me to grow up and look for a respectable woman. But even then, supplying drunk women with more booze and cock and balls wasn't exactly how I thought I could pick up a respectable woman. My options these days were limited.

"Don't play dumb with me, Tito. I know your type. Love 'em and leave 'em. I asked Jay about you. I wanted to know if you were available. He told me he thought so, but he had seen you with several different women over the months. They pretty much come and go when the wind changes. You telling me Jay is a liar?"

"Oh gosh, no! I'd love to explain all of that to you." Lie number two. I dreaded explaining my situation to anyone, especially a potential date. I stood there, shifting my eyes everywhere, except to hers.

"I'm waiting." She tapped her foot on the floor before turning to leave again and calling out behind her, "All men. Boy, bye!"

I fumbled with my words, unable to speak coherently. I had a thousand different ways I wanted to tell her she was wrong. But I wasn't sure that I was ready to put my private life out there in the open yet. I knew it was coming one day, but today wasn't the day.

Instead of running after her again, I bit my tongue and watched her leave.

I pulled up at my dad's place a little after midnight. My eyes burned with exhaustion. Two drunken patrons had needed my help in getting home, so I'd had to call an Uber and see them off safely. Jay had stayed with me the entire night.

We never spoke about Betty again after she left. We had both been too busy. Scarlett Herb continued to grow, and every night lately, we'd been packed. Even our reservations were booking two weeks out. Aiden was scrambling to open a new location, but due to his perfectionism, the search continued.

I had to admit, he thrived in the restaurant business. His creative mind kept Scarlett Herb fresh and new. Jay had the same business sense. Those two together were the dynamic duo of the Outer Forks restaurant world. And me? I was a simple mixologist and moonlighting stripper. I did what I had to do to get by. But one day—and I never admitted this to anyone—I wanted to have my own bar.

It wasn't that I didn't like working at Scarlett Herb. I loved it. The pay was great, the people were terrific, and it was steady work. But I did enjoy crafting cocktails, and I would love to do it on my own terms. Jay and Aiden usually let me create whatever, but it wasn't the same as having my own place. I hadn't quite figured that dream out. I hadn't had the time yet. My personal life consumed me.

I quietly shut the door on my old truck and made my way inside my dad's house. My keys jangled against the lock as I held my breath and tried to silently sneak through the door.

"Daddy!" my daughter, Maisy, cried out.

"What are you doing out of bed, peanut?" I asked.

"Gramps fell asleep again. He was watching TV with me, and he did this thing." She tossed her head back, and with her nose toward the ceiling, she stretched her tiny mouth open, snoring loudly through her throat.

"We're all tired, I guess. But you're going to be the most tired. Your six-year-old little body can't handle being awake for so long. You'll be a terror tomorrow." I rubbed my palm over my face, desperately trying to wake myself up.

"Not me! I don't get tired!" she said, bouncing up and down before tucking herself into a ball and somersaulting across the kitchen.

"Gramps probably hasn't mopped this floor in fifteen years! Get off there! Come on. Let's get you up to bed. I think we're just going to sleep here tonight. I'll bring you back home tomorrow. Maria is watching you." I groaned as I bent over to pick her up and into my arms.

"Not that witch!" she whined, burying her head into my shoulder.

"Maisy! You can't speak that way about people. Maria is a nice lady." Lie number three of the day.

I considered myself an honest person, but sometimes, I dished out the bullshit for everyone else's good.

"No, she isn't, Daddy. Maria makes me go to bed. She won't let me watch TV with her, like Gramps. She's like one of those people in that green stuff."

"What green stuff?"

"The stuff that makes you invisible."

"I've no idea what you're talking about."

"They wear it and fight!"

"Wear it? Do you mean camouflage?"

"Yes." She yawned as I cradled her in my arms, carrying her up the stairs to the spare bedroom.

"So, you're saying she's like an army person? A drill sergeant?"

"That yells and blows whistles."

"Yes, sweetie, that's a drill sergeant." I set her on my old daybed and rolled down the Teenage Mutant Ninja Turtles sheets Gramps had saved from my childhood.

Maisy didn't mind the *boy* sheets. She thought she was too cool for dolls and pink anyway. Somewhere along the line, she'd decided that she didn't want to be thought of like a princess or a baby. She wanted to be treated as an independent child.

I tucked her in snuggly under the blankets and brushed the wild curls from her face before leaning down to kiss her good night.

"Maria doesn't have a whistle though," she mumbled, fluttering her eyes closed.

"No, she doesn't," I whispered.

"Don't buy her one, okay?"

"I won't." I laughed, flicking the lamp off.

"Promise?"

"Promise. Now, get some sleep. The morning will be here before you know it." I tiptoed backward out of the bedroom and shut the door behind me.

My feet dragged as I made my way to the bathroom and readied myself for bed.

Tomorrow night, I'd be working another shift at The Steamy Clam. My dance routine had been growing stale. I needed to up my game if I wanted to remain exciting for the women who stuffed my drawers with cash. But without the energy, I was going to become a washed-up stripper before I could even land a stable, steady gig.

I peered into the mirror in front of me, leaning in to inspect the stubble that I'd grown across my jawline. No matter how hard I tried, I struggled to grow a full beard. But the ladies in the club and at the bar seemed to like my five o'clock shadow just fine.

I brushed my teeth and washed my face, too tired to shower the herbal scent of Scarlett Herb off of me. My hands reached up over my head as I stretched my back and opened the bathroom door.

"You sleeping here then?" my dad, James, asked, tilting his head to the side.

"Jeez! You can't scare me like that! Yes, we're going to stay. Sorry I was late. Drunkards at the bar. Safety first. The last thing the restaurant needs is a lawsuit." I shrugged my shoulders and turned off the light.

"You're working too hard, you know. I don't think you need as much money as you think you need. Maisy will be fine. She has everything. What she needs—" he started.

"Stop. I already know." I threw my hands in the air. "I'm working on it. Hopefully, I can slow down soon. It's just busy season with patio weather. I'm doing my best, Dad. Really, I am. You know it."

"I know. It's hard. Remember, I raised you as a single dad too. When your mom left, I had to bring you to work with me sometimes. I'd wake you up in the middle of the night when I was on call, and you would bring a pillow and sleep in my office." His face drooped as if he'd aged four years just by recalling those memories.

"Yep, I remember. I don't think the strip club or the bar is a place I could bring Maisy. So, what do you suggest? How else do I support her and give her everything I can?"

"Just be with her. She doesn't need the latest and greatest. She'll survive. She only wants you. And maybe a lady friend. You know she needs that. Not one of your eighteen babysitters but someone steady." He put his hands behind his back and leaned into the wall, resting his hip against the striped '70s-style wallpaper.

"No time to date," I groaned. "Plus, whenever I mention that I'm a single dad, women usually run the other way. Just like Jane did and just like Mom." I folded my arms across my chest and rested against the other wall.

It was too late for me to have this discussion, but I knew my dad had been wanting to have this talk for a while.

"Apple doesn't fall far from the tree, does it? You picked a runner, and so did I. But guess what. I got you out of it, and I couldn't be happier. I'd do it all over again in a heartbeat. Your mom was the one who missed out on life. Just like Jane. She's missing the best moments of her child's life by not watching her grow up. That little girl in there"— he nodded his head toward the spare bedroom—"she is special. It doesn't take gadgets and gizmos to show her that either. You're a good dad, and I'm proud of you."

I pushed myself off the wall, ready to end this conversation. "Thanks. She's my world."

"I know. And you both are mine," he said, patting my back as I turned to go. "Now, get some sleep."

I nodded, shuffling my feet down the hall. Since Maisy often slept in the spare bedroom, the only other place for me to lay my head was on the couch in my old game room.

I had slept in this room often as a teenager. When I was old enough to stay home alone, my dad would order pizza, and I'd stay up all night long, playing video games and eating junk while he ran to the office. It certainly beat sleeping in his office while he dialed in to conference calls.

Because I spent a lot of time unsupervised during my teenage years, I got in my fair share of trouble here and there. I didn't blame my dad for not being there all the time. He was there in the moments I needed him. He made sure to support me in every way he could, but times were tough, and like me, he worked a lot. We didn't have much when I was growing up. I survived on bologna sandwiches, cornflakes, and late-night television. That was, until I hit sixteen. Then, my life mostly consisted of girls, beer, and friends who weren't as much friends as they were bad influences.

But still, even through rough times, my dad loved me and let me know that often. When it was time for me to head off to college, he supported me and my decision to major in hospitality. When he learned that I had knocked a girl up, he stepped in and helped Jane and me both financially. He never told me he was disappointed or that I was a failure. He said nothing, only offering to help us when we needed it.

But when Jane had left and I'd had to quit school, that was when I'd learned just how much my father cared. He'd retired as early as he could, and took care of Maisy while I worked odd jobs here and there.

Things were finally beginning to come together with the stability from my mixologist job at Scarlett Herb and my side hustle at the strip club, but I still had nights like tonight that wore everyone out. I had a lot of dad guilt, leaning on my father for help and not being there as much as I wanted to for Maisy. But I needed a steady income and money in the bank so that I could relax and have more time to be a dad one day.

If I could just put my nose to the grind for a few years, Maisy and I and even my dad could all live the good life. I would work my bar and set my hours to have a flexible enough schedule so that I could be there for Maisy. Not to mention, I'd pay myself pretty well, and then I could provide Maisy with something more than a tiny one-bedroom apartment. I'd pack her gourmet lunches for her uppity school, buy her the latest iPhone, and cross my fingers that she had everything she wanted in life and would never rebel against me—or worse, become just like me when I had been a teen.

I just need to win the damn lottery, I thought as I plopped myself on the couch, taking the throw blanket from the back cushions and covering myself.

I cringed at the thought of sleeping on this dirty sofa again. Plenty of times, I'd had girls up here and had to flip the couch cushion to play Hide the Wet Spot before my dad came back home. Those were the good ol' days. Sneaking beer and banging chicks left and right. High school was my golden years, and now, at twenty-eight, my shenanigans were sadly all out of my system. Almost.

THREE

Betty

I pulled The Pink Taco Truck into the parking spot right across from Scarlett Herb. Friday nights at the square were always busy for us. All those drunk people stumbling out of expensive restaurants needed cheap food to eat. After spending a hundred dollars on Jay's pricey-ass cocktails, they couldn't afford his pricey-ass entrees. That was where my DTF gang came into play. Our tacos supplied drunk food up until we sold out or until midnight. We usually sold out before ten.

Our sister truck operated on the other side of town and had been doing just as well. The new employees I'd trained caught on quick and even surprised both Rox and me on how well they'd been doing, taking over the other side of Outer Forks. We operated on the artsy/hipster side of town, and they focused on the university area and the big business/corporate side, which meant that I no longer had to wake up at the crack of dawn and drive this big-ass truck across town. Sometimes, we'd switch it up for a change of scenery, but we usually stuck to our same old spots and routines.

"Where is Layla?" Rox asked, searching in the rearview mirror.

Layla wanted to follow us tonight so that she could leave a little later. Lately, she and Aiden had been hanging out and doing all sorts of things together. That girl was in a heap of trouble. Aiden's Australian accent alone made a tingle in my panties, and I wasn't even attracted to him. It wasn't that he wasn't hot. He was one of the most attractive men I'd ever seen. But he wasn't wild enough for me. Aiden was a businessman who owned a stuffy restaurant, and I liked bad boys who lived on the edge. You know, the ones who needed punishment for heavy-handing my liquor and stripping their clothes off for cash.

"She probably got lost back there. You know her; she's directionally challenged," I said, unbuckling my belt and heading toward the back to start prepping food.

"Well, shit. Nikki's running late too. She just texted me."

"It's just me and you, Rox. Like old times." I smiled, reminiscing on the days so long ago when it had been only Rox and me back at that diner, where I'd met my best friend.

"I guess I can tolerate just you." She laughed. "Hey! Speaking of old times, any word from Earl? It's been about two weeks since he stopped by to eat."

Earl was the reason that our taco truck had been born. He'd believed in us enough to bankroll us into beginning our food truck adventures. Sometimes, all it took was just one person to believe in you. A shining example of that was Rox. These days, she was back to her old self—a badass chick whose smile dazzled even the darkest thoughts out of me. I had to give it to Jay. He had brought life back to my friend when I was worried her ex had sucked it all out of her. I still couldn't believe the drastic change.

"Just a few days ago, he called to make sure all was well. He said he's been looking for a new investment. You know how he is. He has more money than he knows what to do with." I shook my head.

"Sorry I'm late!" Nikki blurted, opening the back door to the truck and climbing inside. "Ma has been all over my ass about this wedding business. She stopped me as I was leaving and had to show me about eighteen bazillion places she'd marked in these damn wedding magazines she'd bought."

"I still can't believe you're going to be a bride," Rox said. "I thought for sure it would be Layla first."

"Speak of the devil," I said as I heard Layla's car door slam shut. I knew it was her because she was OCD and slammed it shut twice. Always. I had no idea why, and I didn't ask questions. It was Layla.

"I don't know how I lost this big-ass pink truck in traffic! My mind must have been elsewhere!" Layla climbed into the truck and tied an apron around her waist.

"We know where your mind is. When are you going to admit it?" Nikki pulled out her phone and started tweeting our location and specials. She was our social media guru, and after her debut as Crystal Cream Pie at the strip club, she'd risen to be an Instagram sensation herself.

"Admit what?" Layla's eyebrows pulled together. She was genuinely confused.

The poor girl was more than a few crayons short of a full box.

"You and Aiden," Rox said.

"When are y'all going to give up on that? Gosh! I promise we're just friends. There hasn't been any hanky-panky!" Layla's cheeks flared red.

"You're as red as my man's ass last night when I whipped the hell out of it. You're lying. Give us the details. You finally got you some of that loving from Down Under, didn't you?" I said, teasing her.

Layla and I always teased each other. It was our love language.

"Whose ass did you smack? Was that in your new sex dungeon?" Layla changed the subject.

"No one's. I was lying. I haven't found anyone worthy yet. But don't change the subject. Tell us what y'all been doing." I pulled out a knife and began chopping lettuce.

I hated food prep. It was the most tedious part of the taco truck business, and I usually put it off for as long as I could. I much preferred dealing with customers, especially the rude ones. They were my specialty.

"Oh, you'll have someone worthy. Maybe even tonight." Rox nodded toward Terrance.

"Shit. What's he want now?" I wiped my hands on a dishrag and hopped out of the truck.

The last thing I needed was DTF teasing me over whatever conversation he planned on having with me. I knew I had treated him pretty shitty yesterday, accusing him of swiping my wallet. But I didn't like to apologize. Call it my fatal flaw or whatever. One of them anyway.

"Coming out here to apologize to me, Miss Queen Betty? Finally figured out that it's not all men?" Terrance grinned.

A tiny dimple on the right side of his face twitched, and I had the sudden urge to put my finger on it and trace it down to those lips of his that curled in a smirk.

"Never. What's up?" I asked.

"Well, let me have the bigger balls here and apologize for something I didn't do. I'm sorry you lost your wallet, Betty. Sorry that happened to you. Also"—he stared down at his shoes before looking up at me with a devilish gaze that made even me, the badass Betty, take a step back—"I want to ask you out. We've been flirting for ages. I think you might have the wrong impression of me. But I want you to have the right one. I know my schedule has been tight lately, but if you're free this weekend, I can make it work. Tomorrow? Can you do that? I'm working at night, but I'm free that afternoon."

"Just what kind of date? Lunch?" My heart thumped hard in my chest.

I hadn't been asked on a date in who knew how long. I only cycled through my friends with benefits when I needed them, which hadn't been much these days. My schedule stayed as busy as Terrance's, if not more. Thankfully, I hadn't had to resort to stripping—yet. Not that I was opposed to it. These boobs could bring in heaps of cash. But working The Pink Taco Truck provided me with what I needed. Now, I just needed to save it all for ... something. One day. I had no idea what that something was, but I trusted it would come to me in time.

"How do you feel about baseball? There's a game," he stammered. His eyes shifted left and right in line with his feet, which couldn't stand still. "I'm kind of involved."

"What do you mean, you're involved?"

The thought of Terrance in tight baseball pants made my heart beat even faster. That was the moment I decided, *To hell with it.* He was going to be my first boy toy to christen my new sex dungeon.

"I coach sometimes. Actually, crap, I can't do that. I forgot. That's the wrong date. How about Sunday instead? Does that work? We can do the typical lunch thing. I'll find a good place. Brunch even, if you're free?" He took a deep breath. The dimple that seemed to wink at me disappeared.

"Sunday brunch. I can do that. Any place in mind?"

"A few. Can I get your number, and I'll text you tomorrow and let you know?" He rubbed the back of his neck, shifting his feet again.

"Sure."

I pulled my phone out of my back pocket, watching him do the same, and told him my number. He typed it on his phone and sent me a text. I stored his info under Stripper Tito because that was what I was going for with Terrance—his alter ego. He was a bad boy, and bad boys who wanted to pull that mischievous shit on me were punished.

"Right. Got it." I tucked my phone back into my pocket.

"Right." He scuffed his foot across the pavement. He glanced around the busy parking lot.

"Anything else?" I asked.

Terrance and I had always been able to cut up and shoot the shit. But this conversation felt awkward. I hoped this didn't mean that when we finally got down to dating or sexing, we were a total dud together in the sack. I'd felt chemistry with him since that day I first sat across from him at his bar. I knew he felt it too.

"Nope. Nada. Zilch. Zero. Nothing else to see here." He cleared his throat and nodded before turning to go, scuffling away as quickly as possible.

I walked back toward the truck, unsure of what had just happened. I knew Terrance had given me his number, and I knew we were going to brunch on Sunday, but I had no idea what had been going through his mind. He'd seemed unsettled. I shrugged my shoulders before climbing back in the truck.

"And?" Rox asked as the entire DTF crew stared at me, waiting.

"We have a date. Brunch on Sunday, I guess. It was just weird. He seemed nervous. Like he wanted to say more but didn't. Must be a White-boy thing. I had that with another one before too." I grabbed the knife and a tomato, getting back to food prep.

"It's not a damn White-boy thing, Betty. It's you. I'd be scared to date you too. I mean, who has a sex dungeon in their own damn house?" Layla tilted her body from side to side in some weird victory dance like she'd just roasted me.

I stopped chopping and pointed the knife in her direction. "I would tell you to watch it, but for once, your dumb butt is right. I'd be scared to date me too."

"What magic is this?" Nikki cried, reaching up to flick a crystal she had hung above the sink. "Betty just said someone is right! Some kind of miracle's going on in here!"

"And by *miracle*, you mean, me not sticking my foot in your ass." I narrowed my eyes until she broke her gaze with mine.

"False alarm. She's still Betty. Carry on." Nikki winked at me.

"Same ol' Betty. Breaking in that dungeon with Terrance," Layla sang.

I sent my foot flying behind me, playfully kicking her in the pants.

"Mmhmm. See? Prepping for an ass-kicking already. You're going to have him on his knees in no time!" Layla laughed, dodging my kick.

"That's the plan," I muttered, finally giving in to the banter. "Tito will be mine."

Rox let out a, "Whoop, whoop," as we all laughed, and I began to speculate how my brunch date would go down on Sunday.

Right after I had made my date with Terrance, I'd called Shay, my hairstylist, for an emergency appointment. If I was trying to get laid and break in my dungeon, I needed to freshen up this mop on my head. Not that my hair looked terrible now, but I needed something new. Thankfully, Shay had said she could squeeze me in first thing in the morning Saturday. Otherwise, my current Afro wouldn't match the femdom black vinyl I planned on wearing once I tied my boy, Terrance, to my bed.

I ran my fingers through my hair and climbed out of my car, noticing a dozen other cars already in the parking lot. The sun had barely come up, and the place was packed full. Shay's Salon was the most prestigious salon for Black women in Outer Forks. Whatever look I was going for, Shay could nail it in a heartbeat. Her skills were unmatched by any other stylist that I'd ever been to, and for that, I paid the price. I had a special fund set up just for my hair. It was called the 'Fro Dough. Not like that little White boy running around in that *Hobbit* movie, but like I needed some cash for my flawless Afro.

I opened the door to the salon. The familiar smell of coconut sent me into a warm and comfortable frame of mind. Shay made her own line of products that were supposedly organic, vegan, cruelty-free, and all that jazz. She'd told me that was the only thing this hipster town would buy these days. And by the looks of all the younger folks in here, I believed her.

At thirty-one, I was the oldest woman here, not counting the two other stylists, Sheila and Sherry. Shay had run both of those ladies out of their home-based businesses. But surprisingly, they had been flexible in giving up their turf to Shay, a bright-eyed young prodigy stomping all over their grounds. I guessed they had known the times were changing, and if they wanted to keep their jobs, they'd have to keep up with the trends. And the Outer Forks Black-hair trend was cutting-edge modern.

No more back room of Sheila's house for the young whippersnappers today. They had given up on Sherry's garage salon as soon as Shay opened her doors. I couldn't blame them. Shay's place looked like something out of a pop-culture magazine. Everything was bright white, except the colorful art prints scattered throughout the room and the bubblegum-pink lights hanging from the ceiling. This place looked much more like New York City than Outer Forks, but the locals loved it. Hence, the packed waiting room.

I grabbed a magazine and made myself comfortable in the only available chair. I squeezed in between two younger ladies with their heads stuck in their phones, no doubt Instagramming their stories of being at the beauty parlor— *ahem*, salon. Even the term *beauty parlor* sounded dated.

Word on the street was that all the boomer Black women had found a salon across town once Sheila and Sherry abandoned ship. Those old ladies had been loyal to their stylists for years because Black women didn't trust their hair with just anyone. When a Black woman had her hair done, she'd better know who was touching it. That trust took years to build. But Sherry and Sheila had sold out, and those stubborn old ladies weren't having it. They had taken their business elsewhere, refusing to set foot in an edgy salon instead of a room that smelled like their grandmama's parlor, where the gossip was just as hot as their straightening combs.

I lost track of time as I flipped through the entire stack of magazines, waiting for my turn in the chair.

"Rumor has it, you're here to impress a White boy, Betty. Come on over here," Shay called out across the salon.

Half a dozen faces turned toward me, grinning, as I made my way toward her chair.

"How do you always know everything around town? I don't get it. He's not just any White boy. He's Tito, the mixologist stripper down at The Steamy Clam," I replied, shutting down all the stares.

"Really? That man is fine!" a younger lady said, meeting my gaze in the mirror in front of her. "The way he dances. Mmhmm! You know he's going to rock your world. I'd be in here, too, if he asked me out." She licked her lips.

"Bet," I said, nodding before settling into Shay's chair.

"A stripper from The Steamy Clam, huh? That's a new one. Even for you." Shay threw the plastic robe over me and immediately began to work.

"New for me? What's that mean?" I held my head straight, fighting against the comb as she brushed the demons out of it.

"You're always going after some outlandish men. Let's see. I know about the stuntman, the hacker, the yogi, the zookeeper, the chemist, and the race car driver. I can't forget about him." She smirked, tugging at my hair harder.

"What's so outlandish about being a chemist?" I asked, folding my arms under the robe.

"Just that he was caught making meth. That's all." She laughed. "Lordy, only you, Betty. Only you."

"You know I never even suspected that, and he was out the door the second I heard. That does seem to be my luck though, doesn't it? He'd better be glad I hadn't heard of that shit before the news broke. I'd have shoved his balls in those beakers and cooked them until they melted. Make him smoke that. Crackhead." My nostrils flared.

That was the most humiliating thing that had happened to me in a very long time. I had been dating him—Mel the meth dealer—for only a short while before his crimes came to light. That had been a terrible mess in my life that I had to clean up. Like I had needed any of that.

I'd learned at a young age not to mess with that shit. My good-for-nothing dad had run us into poverty with his drug abuse, causing my mom to struggle to pay the bills. He'd eventually run away, and I still didn't know whatever had happened to him. I was a stereotype. My dad had left for a pack of cigarettes and never come back. But good riddance because he'd ruined my life when I was growing up. Both mine and my mama's. And after that, she'd kept jumping from one loser to another, trying to save us all. Instead, she had been blind and let them all bring us down.

We hadn't had the money for anything. Forget about getting my hair done. I'd worn an Afro throughout my childhood because natural hair was all I could afford. And back then, Afros weren't in style. Kids had made fun of me throughout my entire time at school. I didn't live in poverty anymore. And I refused to ever even entertain the idea of drugs or debt or anything that could ruin my life.

So, fuck Mel the meth head. He'd almost destroyed my life. I'd never let a man or anyone do that.

I threw my hands out from under the robe, beginning to sweat. Just the thought of Mel had me growing hotter by the minute.

"They all have some type of shit, don't they? Glad you found out he was into that mess before he somehow got you involved. Though I know you ain't dumb enough to go down that road. Miss Betty, queen of The Pink Taco Truck. I hear things have been looking up for you since y'all opened that second sister truck." She stepped back, waiting for me to answer.

"What's with these salons and gossip? Yes, I got a new home, and money is good. I'm good. And my date with the stripper is gonna be good if you make my hair more than good. I need something ferocious. Like I'm going to eat him up—because I am. Let me tell you, Shay. This man has a body like one of them Roman statues. And his face is chiseled perfection too. But he needs to know who he's dealing with. I want a long, lustrous, slightly untamed weave. But also professional so that he and everyone else know I mean business. I'm not playing with these men anymore. Well, I'm playing with them but in my own way. Not being played with. I run this show." I smiled at myself in the mirror, wondering if Terrance could handle me. Probably not. I'd yet to find anyone who could. Sometimes, I couldn't handle myself.

"Oh, girl, I feel ya. You gotta show these men who's boss, and that starts with this crown we wear on our head." Shay tapped the roots of my hair.

"So, let this crown show him that he'd better treat me like a queen or else it's *boy, bye!*" I settled into the chair and watched Shay work her magic.

Sunday morning arrived, and I'd successfully not slept on my new hair last night. I had a crick in my neck, and I was tired as hell, but I didn't care because my hair remained flawless. Shay had nailed my hair, and I readied myself to nail my man.

Terrance had texted me last night, letting me know to meet him at a new place that had just opened up nearby Scarlett Herb. He knew the bartender there, and he would make us a mean Bloody Mary, which just so happened to be my drink of choice. Terrance made them for me often and even added a dash of The Pink Taco Truck's Shizzle Sauce. This new bartender at brunch had a lot to live up to, but I'd give him a chance. If anyone knew their mixology, it was Terrance.

I texted him that I was here as soon as I parked my car. Like the rest of Outer Forks, it was packed. Our small town had grown so much over the last few years that I began to feel overcrowded myself. I was a city girl through and through, but the sudden influx of new residents made traveling in my local area more than frustrating. Businesses boomed, but long wait times and traffic were less than ideal. Our new sister taco truck even struggled to keep up with orders. Earl had mentioned possibly purchasing another or even opening a steady place.

I didn't have time to think about more business. I was already stretched thin, but I wasn't complaining. I liked keeping busy, being busy, and getting busy. And now, my goal was to get busy with my new stripper boy toy, if he could handle all this.

I smoothed my skirt down and pushed my boobs up before entering the building. He texted back, saying that he'd reserved us a corner table and he was there already, waiting.

That's one point for him being on time.

I immediately spotted him from across the room. The way his jaw dropped as soon as he saw me gave me a tickle in my pants. I only needed to flutter my lash extensions at this man, and he would become putty in my hands—and in my dungeon.

FOUR

Terrance

I'd never thought of myself as the nervous type. But the second I saw Betty—or as I liked to refer to her, Queen B—walk through that entrance, I began to sweat so much that I was going to give myself swamp ass just by looking at her. Those wild curls in her hair looked like she could remove one and tie me up with it, which I'd happily be eager to try.

"Morning, Terrance," Betty said, pulling out the chair across from me and sitting down before grabbing the cocktail menu.

"Oh, sorry! I was going to get that for you. I'm just ..." I shook my head. My brain had gone fuzzy the moment I saw her, and already, I was screwing this up.

"You were distracted by my new look. I get it." She smiled sweetly, cocking her head to the side.

Betty never smiled sweetly. Something was going on. My foot began to shake under the table.

"So, Terrance ... Tito ... whatever your name is—"

"Terrance. You know Tito is just the stage name. Like your friend Nikki's stage name, it's my brand. Kind of. Tito isn't me."

A waiter came by to take our order, derailing whatever conversation she had planned to firehose me with.

"I'll try the Bloody Mary, please. And I'll need another minute on the food." Betty searched the menu, nodding her head at the long list of entrees.

I'd checked out the menu online before arriving. Everything here was exactly how I'd imagined it—crafty spins on classic foods. Because that was along the same lines as The Pink Taco Truck's menu, I thought Betty would like it.

Score points for me!

"If I may make a few suggestions, miss?" The waiter clasped his hands together and rocked back on his heels. His button-up looked stiffer than the starched shirts I wore while working at Scarlett Herb.

I shifted in my seat, brushing imaginary—or not so imaginary—crumbs off of my tight-fitting, plain white T-shirt.

"Sure," Betty said. Her eyes lit up as the man rambled off today's specials and their more popular menu items. She looked at me and smiled before returning her gaze to the still-blabbering waiter. "Yum! I think I'd like to try the duck confit and waffles. That sounds interesting."

"And for you, sir?" The waiter looked at me for the first time since I'd been seated.

"The smoked barramundi brandade," I said without any hint of hesitation. I might not have been dressed like I fit into a place like this, but working at Scarlett Herb had taught me all the fancy-schmancy stuff I needed to know about food to dine at this level.

"Wonderful. I'll be right back with your Bloody Marys. Oh, and your hair is stunning." He bowed to Betty before scurrying off.

The corners of her lips twitched, no doubt fighting back a *don't I know it* smile.

"Stunning. Why couldn't I have used that word?" I sighed, grabbing my napkin and setting it across my lap.

"You were awestruck," she muttered.

"I was. You sat down and then I got flabbergasted and then you started talking and I—" My knee bobbed even faster underneath the table.

"And I was about to get down to business before the waiter came. I know; I know. I'm joking with you. Come on. I'm not that much of a hard-ass. Relax. This is just like we're sitting at your bar, having drinks. Don't make it all date-like." She unfolded her napkin and fanned herself.

I wondered if she felt nervous too. If so, she wore a damn good poker face.

"But it is a date," I said, tipping my chin at her in a move that I thought would come off as smooth, but nope. I looked like a douche bag. All I needed now was a pair of sunglasses to wear inside, a chinstrap goatee, and a backward baseball cap. Maybe even a Bluetooth hanging around my neck.

"Yep. Time for me to get to know the man outside of the bars and strip clubs. And why the rumor is that Tito is a playboy womanizer. Is it Tito or Terrance? That is where we left off, right? Do you think I'm that type of girl? To mess with your type?"

"Wow. Going straight in for the kill. I haven't even had a drink yet." I glanced toward the exit, wondering how fast I could make this date. I already felt stupid enough for thinking I could finally open up about my private life—and with her especially.

Hiding Maisy exhausted me. If everyone knew how hard I, as a single dad, really had it, then maybe I could catch a break.

I fought going down that road and explaining my situation to anyone. The judgment would start rolling in when I began telling my friends and coworkers I was a single dad who stripped and served alcohol. But that was the truth. The bills were easily being paid. I wouldn't make the tips I made by sitting in a cubicle.

"What do you need a drink for? Tallying up those women in your head and wondering if I'm worth a notch on that bedpost? How do you know I'm not trying to make you a notch on my bedpost?" Her eyebrows shot up into her hairline.

I rubbed my eyes just as the waiter brought over our drinks.

I took a long sip before clearing my throat and digging my heels into the ground. I had to do this. If I could rip off my secret like a Band-Aid, I would feel much more relieved. Or at least, I thought that was how I would feel.

"Ahem." I gulped. "Those women everyone gossips about, they're my babysitters."

"Like … you have to be watched? You got something wrong with you? A sponsor? Like AA? Why are you drinking, Terrance? What the fuck?" Betty reached over, grabbed my drink, and gulped it down.

"Wait! Damn. You're chugging it! I don't need a babysitter as an AA sponsor. That isn't even close!" I frowned at my half-empty glass.

"Oh good. So, that means you just have one of those baby-diaper kinks. You like to wear diapers and pacifiers and all that? Are they your babysitter, like, in that way?" She handed me back my cocktail. Her nose crinkled up as if she were imagining me sitting across from her, wearing a diaper.

"Jeez, no! Look, I have boxers on. Want me to show you?" I lowered my voice, glancing around at the faces at the tables surrounding us.

Luckily, no one was paying attention to us.

"The babysitters are for my daughter. I have a daughter. Maisy. She's six, and she's my world." I sat up straight and clenched my jaw, prepared for whatever she was about to dish out.

"You, huh? What?" She smacked her lips and downed her cocktail in one long swig before taking a deep breath and looking straight into my eyes.

"I said, I'm a dad. A single dad. Stripping, bartending single dad."

"Mixologist. You're too good to be a bartender, remember?" She squeezed an olive off of her cocktail stirrer and popped it in her mouth.

"Whatever. It's a job. I work two jobs and bust my ass so that I can give Maisy what I didn't have in life. I grew up with hardly anything, and I want to give her everything."

The waiter came to the table with our food and asked if we wanted refills on our drinks.

"Yes!" Betty shouted before lowering her voice to a whisper. "Please."

"Make mine a double, please. Since someone drank half of mine anyway." My voice trailed off along with my gaze.

Yet again, I wanted to run to the exit and never look back. I could feel the heat between Betty and me. It was much like the chemistry we had on the nights she sat at my bar or the nights she came to watch me dance. I thought that was a good thing. Unless I was mistaking that heat for rage, which with women, I'd been known to do.

Hell, women weren't easy to read. Take Maisy's mom, for instance. She'd stuck around the entire pregnancy, seemingly excited about our new life together. But the second she was able to run off, she did. She'd said she couldn't handle this type of life and she never wanted to be a mom. She had tried, but she was afraid she'd only scar our daughter. She wasn't mother material. And to that, I had said, *Good fucking riddance.* I wasn't father material either, but I learned—and quick. I'd never leave Maisy. Ever. And anyone who had a problem with that could also run out of my life.

"Tell me about Maisy. She sounds like a lucky girl to have a dad who works so hard for her," Betty said.

I didn't know if it was the booze talking or Betty, but that was not the reaction I'd expected.

"Really? You aren't about to reach across the table and slap me? That's a pretty big deal that I never disclosed." I pushed my food around on my plate. My appetite disappeared as fast as my cocktail.

"I'm a little surprised that you haven't told Jay or Aiden. They think all those women coming and going are hookups. How many babysitters do you need?" Betty cut into her waffles and let out a moan the second she took a bite. "Damn, this is good."

"I'm surprised you reacted so ... calmly. I haven't told anyone. I just don't feel like answering questions or facing the judgment that comes with being a single dad—much less a single dad who works as a stripper. I want to protect my daughter from all of that drama too. Both of us. I have a hard time finding a babysitter worthy enough for my little girl." I shifted in my seat.

"Are you gonna eat that?" She pointed her fork at my meal.

I shoved the plate toward her and watched her dig in.

"You know, Terrance, I'm DTF," she said in between mouthfuls of my meal and hers. "We're the most nonjudgmental bunch of besties I know. Nikki is a stripper. Rox has been through all sorts of crazy shit. And Layla, she's just out there in left field somewhere. I don't even know how to explain her."

"And you?"

"Pfft. Child, I'm perfect." She took another bite of my breakfast and washed it down with the rest of her Bloody Mary.

I grinned. "I told you my secret. Now, you tell me yours. Not that I don't believe you aren't perfect. But ..."

"Go on. But what?" She tossed her napkin on the table and sat back.

I leaned forward, suddenly brave—or stupid—and looked her straight in the eyes. "But you're hell on wheels.

You look at me as if you're ready to pounce on me and tear me up—and I like it. You're a lioness, and I want to be your prey. You're all woman, and someone like you doesn't get by in life without any secrets." I threw back the rest of my drink so that I could stare at the bottom of the glass and not at her anymore.

I didn't know what had made me say that. It certainly wasn't the alcohol. I wasn't even buzzed. This restaurant's mixologist didn't heavy-hand shit. I guessed the sexual tension Betty and I had shared over the last few months became too much, and I was either a *shit or get off the pot* guy. And right now, I was shitting. Almost literally. I probably did need to wear those diapers she'd mentioned because my dumbass had just sexually harassed the feisty demon, who was sitting within arm's reach of me. My butt clenched tight.

Betty shot her arm straight up into the air and motioned for the waiter. "Check, please!" she called.

"Wait. I'm sorry. Gosh, that was awful. I'm not sure where that came from. Don't go. I apologize. I've got brunch. No worries." I leaned my head back and stared up at the ceiling, cursing myself. My mouth had gotten me in trouble more times than I'd like to admit. This was one of those times.

"Terrance," Betty said, snapping me back to her attention. She rested her elbows on the table and sneered, "You've been a bad, bad boy. I'm not going to tell you my secrets. I'm going to show you. Now, get this damn check dealt with, and let's go back to my lioness's den."

I swallowed hard, took out my wallet, and got us out of there fast.

I drove Betty to her place in my car, as she had downed those Bloody Marys too fast for either of us to be comfortable with her driving. I didn't mind playing chauffeur. I had a hot-ass, wild woman sitting beside me and barking directions while simultaneously reaching over to stroke my cock. The second we'd strapped our seat belts on, she'd commanded me to whip it out. I didn't even hesitate. I'd pulled out every single inch of me. Even my balls, which she cupped in a grip that should have strangled the life out of my erection. It didn't. If anything, her ballsy moves made me even harder.

"House at the end on the left. You're going to pull in the driveway and tuck yourself back in. I don't want to see your dick until I pull it out this time. Got it?" Betty ran her index finger over my shaft, scratching me with her nail. "Are you okay with me playing with you, Terrance? Will you be my toy for a little while? I'm all about consent, so if you ain't ready for this"—she waved her hands across her body—"then that's okay. You just tell me. Otherwise, I'm going to show you a side of Betty you won't ever be able to forget. You have to trust me though."

"Queen B—that's who you're showing me. It's what I always like to call you in my head. Show Tito how it's done, Queen B. I've known you long enough to trust you on this." I breathed heavy, putting the car in park and tucking myself back into my pants.

"Quick learner," she said, smirking a devilish grin. "I'll start slow."

"Please don't," I growled.

I noticed her nipples had hardened beneath her top. I'd dreamed of sliding my cock in between her big breasts dozens of times. At Scarlett Herb, whenever she proved a point, she performed a boob drop. It was much like a mic drop, but way more … Betty. Her friends always cheered her on when she pushed her boobs up and let them fall into place. Apparently, it was her signature move—and one I'd jerked off to plenty.

"Follow me then."

I walked behind her, silently admiring her juicy ass. Finally, I'd get to see it. I'd never imagined I'd have brunch with a side of Betty today. I'd thought for sure she was going to run the other way at the mention of my daughter. But instead, here we were, walking into her house and straight to her bedroom. At least, I thought it was her bedroom until she opened the door.

"Welcome to my dungeon. In here, I'd usually tell you to call me master. But I can be your Queen B. I like that. Are you ready, Tito? I think Tito needs to be punished. Always up on that stage, tempting women with your goods," she said, gripping my dick, "but never following through. Such a tease." She pulled a whip from out of nowhere and smacked my ass before I realized what had happened.

"Where did that come from?"

"Hush." She smacked me again, making me growl. "Go sit on that swing. I'll be right back."

I took a deep breath and walked over to the swing, passing shelves of contraptions that scared the living daylights out of me yet excited me, all at the same time. I wanted to ask her what the long string of big metal balls was for, but I was afraid to find out. I cringed, imagining where she'd stick them.

I completely undressed and settled into a surprisingly comfortable sex swing. Ready as ever for this wild ride, I took the liberty of buckling my ankles into the restraints that tied to the metal beams.

This must be how women feel at the gynecologist's office, I thought while lying spread eagle, swinging in the air, completely vulnerable.

I hoped she didn't have one of those stretcher things lying around to shove up there. I nervously glanced around, looking for any signs of torture devices. Nothing looked too scary, except for the huge dildos and I was pretty sure those were for her.

Pretty sure, I told myself as I sat, waiting on Betty to come out of the room she'd disappeared to. I assumed it was a bathroom or the gates of hell. It could go either way with her.

As if she could read my thoughts from the other side of the wall, she flung back the door and stepped out in a black vinyl catsuit, which fit her so tight that I had to do a double take to make sure it wasn't a second skin. She sauntered over to me, passing by a row of whips and grabbing two of them. She picked a blindfold off the shelf, some black earbud-looking things, and a condom from a fishbowl jar.

"Safety first." She cackled, throwing the sex toys on a side table before cracking her whip in the air. She swung that thing around like she'd been born to beat the living crap out of someone.

I gulped back my fear and manned up by puffing my chest and my chin out. She ran her fingertips over my naked body, walking around me and tying my hands to the other beams. My limbs were outstretched like a starfish. There was no escaping now.

"I see you're ready." She ran her fingertips along my naked body. "Let's try some sensory deprivation. All but touch and taste. You've been a bad boy. Never even told me your last name." She tightened the restraints around my wrists and kicked two stools out from under me.

"Carter. And yours?"

"Did you just ask Queen B a personal question? No questions. Speak when spoken to. That's all you need to know right now. Enjoy."

She reached to the earbuds sitting on the table and stuck them in my ears until the entire room went silent. The only sound I could hear was my rapid heartbeat beating against my eardrums, as if it were knocking them down to escape this torture chamber.

I opened my mouth to ask a question but closed it just as quickly, remembering she'd said no questions allowed. I didn't want her to get those metal balls out on me. Not yet anyway.

I watched her as she waved good-bye before slipping the blindfold over my eyes. Now, I was in trouble. I couldn't see what was coming, and I couldn't hear what was coming. But by the feel of vinyl straddling either side of my cheeks, I was about to taste what was coming.

I licked my lips, preparing myself as she lowered herself onto my face. She must have a slit in the crotch of her outfit because I received both a mouthful of Betty and vinyl.

She rocked her hips back and forth while I ran my tongue up her soft lips. She moved from side to side, but every few seconds, she'd put more of her weight down on my face, smothering me into her as if she were trying to stuff me back up in there—into the motherland.

I bucked against the restraints, ravenous to find out what she felt like already. By now, my mouth, cheeks, and jaw were wet with her. I had never tasted a woman who melted like slow-dripping honey down the back of my throat. The old saying was true: *the blacker the berry, the sweeter the juice.*

I'd never been with a Black woman before, and now, all I could think of was, *Why the hell not?*

I dived my tongue inside of her as far as it would go while she bounced on my lips. She sat down hard on my face, depriving me of yet something else—breath. I didn't care. I didn't need to breathe. What I needed was for her to touch my dick. The poor thing had been standing on end, wiggling around as if it were one of those snakes that danced to the tune of a flute. How I wished she'd play my flute. But I had a feeling that this charade was all about taking what she wanted. She'd admitted herself that she wanted to use me as her sex toy.

I began to get into this whole face-sitting thing when I felt her rise up and leave. I couldn't hear or see what was coming next, but my asshole clenched anyway.

Touch my dick. Touch my dick. Please touch my dick.

She took out my earbuds, lifted my mask, and held a phone to my ear.

Is this part of the fun? Am I supposed to dirty-talk into this thing or something?

"Hello? Terrance?" my dad's voice called from the other side.

"Um ... oh. Hi, Dad." My jaw dropped.

Betty held the phone, impatiently waiting on my conversation. My dick swayed, flopping over and limping to the side like an untied balloon someone had let go into the air, wildly farting around until falling down in a lame lump of useless pecker.

"Jeez, son! What are you doing? This is my tenth call! You need to come to Outer Forks North Hospital."

"What?" My body convulsed against the ropes. "What's wrong? Maisy?" My heart pounded against my chest.

Betty reached around with her other hand and began to loosen my restraints.

"She hurt her arm. She's fine now, but she wants you. Maria and I are up here with her."

"On my way." My heart lurched.

I'd read one time that when you made a choice to have a child, you chose to live the rest of your life with your heart outside of your body. It was true.

Panic fluttered in my chest, causing me to shiver and tug against the restraints. I pulled my ear from the phone, nodding for Betty to hang it up.

"You okay? Is Maisy okay?" Betty pulled at the ropes, freeing my hands so we could both work on the ankle straps.

"She's at the hospital. She hurt her arm. I'm going to kill Maria! She was supposed to be watching her!" I picked my clothes up off the floor and shuffled into my pants.

"Come on. I'll drive." Betty stripped her catsuit, ran into the bathroom, and came back out, fully dressed, before I even thought of how to respond to her.

I never introduced Maisy to any women I dated. Ever. No sense in her getting attached to someone who wouldn't hang around for long. Thankfully, she didn't remember her mama running, but I wasn't taking any chances on someone breaking her heart. I already dreaded the day she came home crying from school because some douche bag had dumped her. My fists tightened at the thought of her getting hurt.

"Can I have your keys?" Betty asked. "Remember, you drove me. My car is still at the restaurant. I can have Rox pick me up at the hospital."

"Are you sure? I can go by myself. It's fine. I'm fine," I lied. My hands shook. I stuffed them into my pockets, so she wouldn't notice.

"Boy, please. Don't lie. I had you tied up, and then you got some awful news. You're a nervous wreck. You can't even drive. I'm looking at ya. Your eyes are bugged outta your head, and your face is as white as that pale ass you need to tan. Now, give me the keys, and let's go. Besides, I'm fully sober now anyway."

I tossed her the keys from my pocket and followed her to my car. I was nervous but not too nervous to notice what I'd missed on the way up to her dungeon. Her living room was spotless and orderly. The only items that seemed out of place were two dirty glasses sitting on a bar cart next to a record player. I wondered who she had been playing music and mixing drinks for. It had to have been someone special. I hadn't gotten music and drinks. I'd gotten tied up instead.

I felt a slight twinge of jealousy sear through my veins before I quickly remembered my reality. I didn't have time to feel anything other than the pain my daughter was experiencing. I shuddered, running after Betty and into my car.

"Is she at Outer Forks North Hospital or a different one?" she asked, slamming my car door shut.

"Yes. She's at North." I strapped in as she spun the tires out of her driveway. I should have known she was a wild driver. I didn't think there was anything boring or vanilla with Betty.

We drove in complete silence. The hospital was about a twenty-minute trip from Betty's house, but with the way she drove, I knew we would arrive sooner.

"I'm sorry I cut things short. It's just … Maisy. She's … I have to—" I started.

"Hey, Terrance, you don't have to explain yourself to me. That's your daughter. You reacted in the way you should have. She's first. Don't think anything of it. We can do that again another time. Let's go get Maisy!"

She pushed her foot on the gas pedal, sending us back into our seats while she weaved in and out of traffic. I reached up, grabbing the *oh shit* bar above the window, and hung on tight until we made a few quick turns into the hospital parking lot and pulled into an empty space.

"Let's go!" She tossed me the keys and hopped out of the car. Her heels clacked on the pavement in front of me.

"Where did you learn to drive like that?" I asked, running to catch up to her.

"I dated a race car driver once. He showed me some things."

Records and mixed drinks, race car driver showing her some things …

It sounded to me like Betty had a fulfilled life or past or experiences or whatever. She had another layer—or five— I wanted to learn about. Even if the thought of her with another man already, oddly enough, made me feel a little jealous. I had never seen her with other men the entire six or so months we'd been flirting at the bar and club. But I wasn't exactly innocent either. If we compared numbers, I was pretty sure I would come out on top. But then again, maybe not. I didn't have a sex dungeon in my house.

"Maisy Carter, my daughter, is here with a hurt arm. Can you please tell me where she is?" I said to the nurse, fighting out the words between breaths.

My nerves were getting the best of me, and so was my dad guilt. I'd been fucking around with Betty instead of playing with my own child at the park. If I had been there, this wouldn't have happened. I always watched Maisy like a hawk.

"Room 201. Down the hall, on the right," the nurse replied, not bothering to look up from her computer.

Betty grabbed my arm and steadied me as we flew down the hall and into room 201.

"Daddy!" Maisy jumped up before flinching and sitting back down. Her arm was wrapped in a red cast, her favorite color. "Look," she said, trying to hold it up but flinching again before giving up and lying down on the hospital bed. "It's red for Gryffindor. Because I'm brave. I didn't even cry when it happened." Her bottom lip trembled as she stared up at me. Maria cleared her throat. "Well, maybe just a little. Like this much." She held her tiny fingers up and pinched them together.

"It isn't broken. Don't worry. It's strained slightly, but Maisy insisted on a cast. And you know Maisy; what she wants is what she gets. The doctor said she'd be fine to wear it for a few days even though she really doesn't need it," my dad said.

"I know you have questions," Maria began, "but she jumped off the top of the slide. I'd had my eyes on her, as always. She was playing with a little boy up there and said he wouldn't leave her alone. She said she had no choice but to jump because he was blocking the slide. I didn't see that, but—"

"Aw, honey." Betty walked over to Maisy and sat down beside her. "You mean to tell me that Slytherin wouldn't let you pass?"

I shot a look at my dad, who was standing near the top of the bed. His head tilted as he looked from Betty to me and back again. The corners of his mouth twitched in that damn genetic giveaway we both carried when we fought to keep from showing our emotions.

"Mmhmm." Maisy sniffled.

"Now, coddling a child won't toughen her up. She needs a rigid backbone." Maria folded her arms across her chest and stared down at Betty.

Betty narrowed her eyes at Maria. "All girls, boys, everyone needs a backbone. But there's a time and place to teach that. It's not in the hospital room when the poor thing is laid up in the bed with a broken arm." Betty smoothed Maisy's hair back as she sniffled again.

"It's not broken," Maria said through gritted teeth. "Seems to me like you all got this though. I'll be heading out." She turned on her heel and stomped out of the room.

"I think you made her mad," Maisy whispered to Betty. "She's a Slytherin too."

"That's okay. She's also an adult, and she can handle her own emotions."

"Yep, I'm still learning that. Daddy's been teaching me to be mindful and about what to do when I get sad and angry. And also how to tell people how I feel, no matter what. Like this. You're pretty. I like your hair. Are you my dad's girlfriend? What house are you in?" Maisy lowered her voice and shut her eyes tight. "Please don't say Slytherin. Please don't say Slytherin."

"Whoa, slow down there, kiddo." My eyes pleaded with my dad for help. "Did they give her something for the pain, Dad?"

He blinked and nodded, biting his lip to hold back a laugh.

"I'm not Slytherin. I'm a Gryffindor too. Brave and sometimes stubborn. Okay, a lot of times stubborn. But want to know something?"

Maisy nodded her head.

"I know plenty of Slytherins, too, and they aren't all bad. But if ever that little boy or anyone blocks you and makes you feel unsafe or tries to hurt you in any way, you scream, *Expecto a beatin'!* Then, you kick him hard in his quaffle balls and run to an adult for help. Got it?"

My dad bent over, grabbing his sides, and let out a laugh so loud that all three of us jumped.

"Dad, meet Betty. Betty, meet my dad, James. Maisy, this is Miss Betty. Miss Betty, this is Maisy. All right, everything is cool, and we're going to get Miss Betty a ride home. Thank you for helping me out. I've got it from here." I pursed my lips and motioned for Betty to follow me.

"Betty can't stay?" Maisy whimpered.

"Is it because I said quaffle balls?" Betty narrowed her eyes at me.

"Those the things you beat with sticks in quidditch right, Miss Betty?" Maisy perked up and even bounced a little in the bed.

My dad snort-laughed before walking to the corner and plopping himself down into the chair in hysterics. "I'm not touching this one," he said, wiping tears from his eyes.

"Thanks for the help," I muttered. "Maisy, I'll be right back. I'm going to walk Miss Betty out."

"But can she come to check on me tomorrow? My arm hurts so bad." Maisy frowned, lying back on the bed again and wiggling her cast.

"We'll see. I think you'll be a lot better tomorrow though."

Betty smiled at Maisy. "Nice to meet you, sweetheart. I hope you feel better. Remember, you're strong and brave. You're a Gryffindor lion!" She roared, snatching at the air with fake claws.

"Roar!" Maisy called back, swiping her good hand across the air.

Betty waved good-bye to my dad and shuffled outside of the room.

"I'm sorry. Doesn't she know boys have those parts? You gotta teach her! Boys are vicious. She can get in a lot of trouble one day. She has to know how to defend herself. You think you can be there when things like that happen all the time?" Betty rested her hand on her hip.

"No, no, I don't." I pressed my palms into my eyes and groaned. "I'm just not ready yet. And I could have been there today. But I wasn't. I—"

"Was fucking me," Betty replied, shifting her eyes behind me, toward the exit. "It takes a village, Terrance. I admire you. I really do. But it takes a village. Sorry about little Maisy." She pulled her phone out of her pocket and flipped through her Contacts. "I'm sure Rox will be able to get me. You go back in there with your girl. I'm going to get some fresh air. I'll see you around." She stepped around me and walked toward the entrance.

"Hey!" I called out after her.

She stopped mid-step before slowly turning back toward me.

"Thank you." I smiled.

She raised her hand in the air, curling her fingertips into a claw, and swiped the air before baring her teeth into a grin and turning to leave again.

I watched her ass bounce away until she disappeared behind the double doors. I sighed and looked up at the ceiling. I'd experienced enough emotions today to last me the entire year.

"Daddy! I like her," Maisy said, peeking from around the corner.

I do too, kiddo. I do too.

I shook my head and forced myself back into my father role, giving up on my love life for now.

I only had time for one girl in my life, and she wasn't going to have anything broken because of me—especially that tiny heart of hers.

FIVE

Betty

I finally rolled out of bed after hitting the Snooze button on my phone's alarm eight times. Yesterday had drained me. One minute, I'd been about to give Terrance the ride of his life, and the next, I'd been at the hospital, playing Mother Goose to his little girl, who clearly needed a strong female in her life. I had played that role plenty in my nieces' lives, my friends' lives, and even my mama's life. I was no stranger to being tough.

Growing up in poverty had forced me to grow a thick skin. When I'd gone to school, wearing the same clothes day after day, kids had noticed. And kids could be assholes. My defense mechanism had been to develop a shell or walls. I'd always had walls with people. My walls were made of steel. But I had a soft spot for the next generation of girls. I couldn't let innocent little girls grow up and turn out like so many women I'd had to help pick up off the ground because of their ruthless men.

I wanted to show them independence, strength, and bravery, just like little Maisy had mentioned. I'd learned the hard way. We had to take care of ourselves because no one was going to do it for us.

"Did you really tell that little girl to kick that boy in the nuts?" Rox *asked when I explained to her the entire story.*

She'd picked me up from the hospital straightaway.

"Of course I did! He had backed her into a corner, bullying her. You of all people know what that's like." I settled down into Rox's passenger seat and rolled my eyes. "Besides, I didn't say his testicles. I said quaffle balls. I put some Harry Potter in there. I made it kid-friendly."

Rox *laughed. "Oh, yeah? Betty is kid-friendly now. After you told me Terrance had a kid, I thought I'd heard it all. But now, I have!"*

I blew out a breath. "Me too."

"Does it bother you? I know you like him. You're trying to hide it, but I can see a smile behind that resting bitch face of yours. What are you going to do now? You okay with him having kids?"

"First of all, he has a kid. Not kids. One, I can handle. I think. Any more than that, and it would have been a hard pass. She reminded me of my nieces anyway. I don't think she will be a problem. I'm not saying I want to play mother hen. I sure don't want to take care of anyone—yet. But it's not a deal-breaker. To be honest ..." I sat up in my seat and stared at Rox. "Tell anyone this, and I'll cut you. But, to be honest, when he told me his little girl was his world, that was what attracted me to him and made me want to jump his bones. Not his flirting. Though that wasn't bad either. And then, when he ran to her rescue, well, I'll just say, I'm still feeling him out. He's not cut off—yet."

"So, you do like him." She smirked. "Better not tell Layla. She's going to have you taking mommy-and-me classes before you know it."

"Oh, hell no. It'd better be a self-defense class or something. I'm not going to braid hair. Besides, I have no idea what to do with White people's hair. I'll take her to the salon."

"Layla will teach you." Rox side-eyed me and shrugged.

"As far as I'm concerned, nobody is going to know Terrance's business, except Terrance, me, and you. I'll let him tell the world he's been hiding his kid. Not me and especially not Layla."

"You don't want me to tell Jay? Because he still thinks Terrance is a player with all those women coming and going."

"Terrance said they were his babysitters. I'm sure not all of them." I rolled my eyes. "But I did meet one of them, and she was a ripe old bag. The least I can do is steer him in the direction of someone worthy of Maisy."

"Worthy of Maisy, eh? It seems to me like she's already growing on you."

"Nah. You know me. And DTF. We're always trying to save the girls. Support the girls. Raise the girls. Wouldn't it have been nice to skip all the drama and life lessons we had to learn, all those broken pieces, if someone had just taught us from the get-go how to live?" I stared out the window.

"And that's what I love about you. You're the toughest woman I know, and you radiate that strength to everyone around you. You're going to be a good stepmom. The best!" She reached over and squeezed my knee.

"Rox, you do know I have that torture chamber upstairs, right? Remember, in the room that used to be your safe sanctuary? I'm going to invite you over for dinner and give you a lesson in that chamber if you keep talking all that smack." I picked my boobs up and let them drop before throwing my hands up in the air.

"Sounds kinky. Can Jay come too?" She shimmied her tiny chest in response.

I parked The Pink Taco Truck outside of Forks University today. With fall in the air and the students cramming for exams, it seemed like a win-win for the business. All those kids studying should be ravenous for cheap eats, and we were cheap.

My phone had dinged in my pocket two hours ago, but the lunch rush had us so busy that I forgot to check it until I took a break. I half-expected it to be a booty call from one of my many playboys or maybe even Terrance updating me on his little girl. But instead, I'd received the most bizarre text message from my aunt. The old coot was more like me than I liked to admit. She was independent, ruthless, and downright ballsy.

> *Aunt May: I got married. We're having a get-together at my place next weekend. Saturday the 11th. This ain't ever going to happen again. So, you'd better be there, so I can see you before I die.*

I read the text message four times before I could respond. If there was anyone on this earth I'd thought would never marry again, it was my aunt May. She had dumped her ex-husband long ago and vowed never to take care of another man again. I'd always admired her for sticking to her decision, but when her kids had grown up and moved away, I'd realized that she might change her tune. It was tough to always be alone, but being elderly and alone seemed terrible.

DTF and I had a pact that we would be much like *The Golden Girls* when we were as old as my aunt. But lately, the DTF gang had been committing to men left and right. And now, with even my elderly aunt married, I would soon be the only one left alone.

> *Me: Is this a joke?*

I wondered if my aunt was going senile and thought it was April Fools' Day. She was that type of prankster. It would be just like her to pull some stunt like this for attention. She'd get us all out to Memphis and then guilt-trip us for having to lie to get us to visit her.

Aunt May: What? You don't think someone can love this old love sack? Well, he does. Surprisingly. I hope you can make it.

A picture popped up on my screen of her and a gray-headed man smiling at the camera. My aunt was smiling. Smiling!

What the hell?

Me: I'll see what I can do.

I walked out of the taco truck and dialed my mother's number. I didn't speak to my mother very much, let alone see her. I could admit that I held resentment for having to raise my sister and what felt like her too. I could never count on her, even now. She was too busy doing whatever the hell she wanted. She picked up odd jobs here and there, but most of her time was spent being off with this douche bag and that douche bag. They stole money, got her involved in messes, and always left her high and dry. That was when she would come crawling back to me, the tough one, yet again.

One too many times, I'd heard her say how she just wasn't a good mother and never even planned on having kids. She hadn't had my sister and me until her late thirties, and she claimed us both as accidents. It wasn't until my teenage years that I'd begun to realize how toxic relationships worked, and I distanced myself. She'd always be my mama, but I knew trouble when I saw it, and my mama was trouble.

"Well, if it isn't my *too cool for school* child. What is it you need? I only hear from you when you need something," my mother said after picking up on the second ring.

"I can say the same thing, Mama. I take it, you got that check I sent you?" I paced back and forth on the sidewalk.

Rox stuck her head out the back of the truck, checking on me, but I waved her away.

"I did. Thanks." Her voice fell flat.

I knew she had a difficult time with thanking me. Her pride was just one of her many downfalls. But still, she was family, and I'd always take care of her even if it had to be from a distance.

"Good. I was calling about Aunt May though. She said she got married. Are you going to her get-together?" I asked, closing my eyes and praying to God she wasn't.

"And where am I supposed to get money for a plane ticket? Pull it outta my ass?"

You could stop giving it to every lowlife man who uses you for it, I thought.

If my mother had one redeeming quality, it was that she never partook in the drugs and bullshit. But she still let the ones who did ruin her life and mine.

Sometimes, I wondered, *If my dad had stayed, would things have been better?* Maybe one deadbeat dad might have been better than the handfuls of them my mom kept trying to replace him with.

I kept telling myself that my mom was my mom, and she meant well. She was just another one of those little girls who hadn't learned her life lessons quickly enough. Hopefully, I was going to break that cycle with my children one day.

"I can buy your plane ticket, Mama." My stomach churned.

I wanted to help, but I didn't want to give an inch because she would take the five miles she usually did.

"I'll think about it and let you know," she said. I heard a man's voice in the background and rolled my eyes. "Gotta go, baby."

"Bye." I sighed, stuffing the phone back into my back pocket.

I rubbed my eyes and turned my face toward the sun. The heat beamed down hot on my skin. I wanted it to burn and melt away all the emotions that played across my expression. I didn't want to talk about my mom or my aunt.

And I knew Rox and the girls would know something was up if I wasn't my usual chatty self.

"Betty!" a small voice called.

I jumped in response and turned around to see Maisy running toward me, Terrance following closely behind.

"Maisy? Terrance? What are y'all doing here? How's your arm?" I bent over, inspecting her red cast.

Already, she had five signatures on it.

"It's all better! Will you sign it?" She stuck out her hand, gripping a black marker. "Daddy said you could. Said we could get lunch and you could sign it at the same time. He said you made the best tacos. Did you know that's my favorite food? Most kids like pizza. Or apples. Or bananas. Or Oreos. I like those too. But tacos are my favorite. He thought it would cheer me up. But want to know something? You cheer me up," Maisy rattled off, hopping from one foot to the other.

I took her marker and signed my name where she was pointing, right under her dad's name.

"Maisy! Give her time to think at least." Terrance's eyes grew wide while his daughter droned on and on. "I had to bring her. She wouldn't stop asking about the pretty lady who was going to teach her how to Judy chop."

"Judy chop?" I asked her.

"Like this. And a Judy chop!" Maisy jumped up, spun around, and chopped her hand through the air.

"Don't ask. My dad has way too much time to spend on the internet. He showed her some viral video thing. And now, she thinks she's a kung fu ninja. Just what I need. More risk of her getting hurt." Terrance crossed his arms and rocked back on his heels, staring Maisy down.

"He's one of those helicopter parents." Maisy pursed her lips.

I threw my head back and laughed, startling the sassy little spitfire.

"Yet more wisdom from my dear, old dad. Anyway, how about some tacos, kiddo? Let's grab some and go. Miss

Betty is probably super busy." Terrance motioned for us to head to the front of the truck's order window.

"No, she's not. There isn't anyone here. Look." Maisy stuck her hand to her brow and turned her head left and right as if she was searching high and low to prove her point.

"I've got a little break. How about you tell me what you want, and I'll get it? There are a few tables around front. Go have a seat, and I'll be right out."

"Thanks. Just regular tacos. No tomatoes. Sweet tea." Terrance sighed. He looked as if he hadn't slept all night.

"Tomatoes are disgusting! Pickles too. Also, snails. Did you know people eat snails?" Maisy started up again.

"I won't serve you snails. Promise." I looked back at Terrance. "And for you?"

"Whiskey. Valium. Vacation. One of those breaks like you were talking, except about two days long. Minimum," he replied, dragging his feet toward a table.

"I'll see what I can do," I said before heading back into the truck.

"Harry Potter World!" Maisy jumped up and down, following behind her dad.

I felt DTF's eyes on me before I saw them. I knew they'd all been staring out the window, and now, I'd have to answer questions. Sure enough, Layla was the first to open her mouth.

"You're going to be a mommy." Layla jumped up and down, slightly jostling the truck.

I rolled my eyes. "No one said anything about motherhood. Now, make me some tacos without tomatoes." I poured sweet tea into a cup and put a lid on it. Already in mom mode.

"But that's his daughter, right?" Nikki asked. "It has to be. They look so much alike!"

I sighed, staring at Terrance and Maisy out the window. They had their heads together in deep conversation. Maisy kept nodding her head up and down, and Terrance kept shaking his.

"Yes, it's his daughter. Before y'all start asking questions, he's a single dad, not a playboy. He has a few babysitters he uses, which is where all the women you see him with come into play. One, in particular, is a witch."

"Maria?" Nikki looked from Maisy to me and tilted her head.

"How did you know?" I set the cup down and searched her eyes for a clue that she had known all along how Terrance had a child.

"I sometimes saw him paying an older lady outside the back of the club. Same with him paying women I saw coming from his bartending job, too, at Scarlett Herb. Honestly, I thought he was a gigolo, and they were exchanging money or something he owed them. Anyway, he introduced me to Maria one time when she showed up after my gig. She scowled at me and stuck her nose in the air. I didn't ask questions. You know I never do. I thought it was just his business. But now, paying babysitters makes a lot more sense. Damn! Terrance is a single-dad stripper. That's a stereotype turned on its head! Guess we're supporting single dads." Nikki scraped her palms together as if she were throwing money and making it rain.

"Let's let Betty go handle her business. That poor little girl out there with the cast is waiting on her tacos." Rox grabbed the plate from Layla and put one of our choco tacos on it before covering it in sprinkles and whipped cream and handing it to me. "Here. Maybe this will make her feel better. She gets this choco taco, and Terrance will be getting some of your choco taco once he sees how sweet you are to his baby girl."

"And here I thought, you were just being nice. I see how it is, Rox. I don't need to bribe a man to take my goodies. My choco taco is doing just fine. F-I-N-E," I lied. I needed to get laid. After being interrupted during my torture session with Terrance yesterday, I still hadn't had the time to finish myself off.

"Go, go, go, little mama. Then, come back and tell us more." Layla handed me a clump of napkins and shooed me out the door before I could give her my death stare or a playful smack on her ass. She was so used to them now that she would see them coming and stick her butt out, waiting for me to whip it good. I thought she liked it.

I walked a plate of tacos over to Maisy and sat down beside her.

"What is this?" Her eyes grew big at the sight of dessert.

"A chocolate taco. Don't worry. It's not meat. It's ice cream in there. So, eat up before it melts."

"I can have dessert before my meal then?" She looked up at Terrance with puppy-dog eyes, which even shot a warm feeling through my cold, dead soul.

"Yes. Just this once. We wouldn't want it to melt and get too messy. Go ahead. You eat and let Betty and me talk for a bit, okay? We need to have a grown-up conversation. We'll be at that table right there. Five minutes," Terrance said, pointing at a table just a few feet away.

Maisy nodded, her mouth already full of whipped cream. I pushed the pile of napkins toward her and followed Terrance to the other table.

"Look, I want to apologize for all the craziness. For yesterday and bringing Maisy by today without even giving you a courtesy call. It's just that I didn't even know what to say. I'm so damn tired right now; I can't even think straight." He ran his hand through his hair and moaned. "And"—he lowered his voice—"I fired Maria."

I scooted closer so that I could whisper back, "You fired her? She seemed like a mean old lady, but now, what are you going to do? Can your dad watch her more?"

Terrance scooted in even closer, knocking his knee against mine. I instinctively rose my ankle up the entire length of his leg and bit my lip before I realized what I'd done. His eyes grew wide as he glanced over at Maisy, who was stuffing her face and paying us no attention at all.

"Shit! Sorry. I didn't mean to feel you up out here. I mean, I did. Obviously. But that was, like, a reflex. No idea where that even came from." I felt the heat rise in my cheeks, and I thanked God for making me Black.

The last thing I wanted Terrance to know was that Queen B was embarrassed or weak or completely losing herself around him. It wasn't often that happened with me, but when a man wore a tight-fitted T-shirt and had bulging biceps, just like Terrance, I wanted to take a bite out of him. Maisy had diverted my attention, but now, with her out of my sight, I drank up the hot piece of ass in front of me.

"It's okay." He grinned, showing me a bright white smile.

It was the same devilish smile he gave all the women at the club. That smile earned him the big bucks. I'd seen ladies stuffing twenties in his G-string left and right when he grinned like that.

"I'm sorry you have a lot going on. It's okay. I get it. Not that I have kids, but I come from a single mom, and I pretty much ran the house at a young age. That's why I said, it does take a village. I can't help with much, but if you need to get away for a day or two, I might be able to make that happen."

He bit his lip and glanced at Maisy again, who was finishing up her plate.

"What are you saying? A make-up date? We going to do the swing again?" He raised one eyebrow and rubbed his stubbled chin.

Again, I instinctively reached out, stroking his jawline, before realizing what I was doing.

"I don't know what the fuck is wrong with my hands, but I can't keep them off of you. I'd love to finish what I started in my dungeon. Give you some of that Queen B. But this weekend, I have to go to my aunt's in Memphis. I'm flying out just for an overnight. I know you said two days, minimum, but I can't handle my family that long. So, do you want to take a day-long vacation or what? It's not the beach or somewhere exotic. Actually, it is exotic because it's my crazy-ass family but—"

"Yes. I'll go home and pack now. Tell me which flight, and I'll book the tickets. Let's go. Let's get out of here. I need to double-check that my dad can watch Maisy, but I have a feeling he'd jump through hoops for you. He liked you. I do too." He shifted his eyes back to his daughter again.

"Okay. I didn't know if you'd think that was too weird, me asking you to meet my family when we haven't even screwed yet, but here I am. I could see it in your eyes. You need a break. Don't ever feel guilty about it either. I have seen a lot of single parents burn out and give up. We'll make it fun and restful. I'll bring my toys." I rose from my chair. I needed to get out of here and think about the crazy commitment I'd just made.

Am I crazy? What just happened? Why the hell did I invite this stripper man to my family's get-together? Do I really want him to meet my aunt May? Or worse, my mom?

Panic bubbled in my chest as I remembered I needed to call my mom. I hoped she would say she wasn't going to go. I couldn't think of a worse situation than being stuck on a trip with my mom and Terrance. No doubt she would not be happy that I was dating a White boy unless he was super rich. If she learned that he was a stripper, I'd never hear the end of it. She was the last person who needed to be judgmental, but she was the worst when it came to picking people apart.

He followed behind me while I made my way to Maisy.

I quickly turned around, putting my index finger on his soft lips and slowly running it down, past the ripples on his abs and down to his belly button. I couldn't stop myself.

"We'll see how you can punish me with your toys when you can't seem to keep your hands off me now." He smirked.

"It's talk like that that's going to get you in trouble," I snarled.

"Bring it on then, Betty," he snarled back, stepping into me.

My breath caught in my chest. I loved it when a man fought back.

"Daddy?" Maisy came up behind me and stepped between us.

"Hey! Finish your food?" He reached out and pulled her to him, hugging her tight.

"Yes. And I did this!" She stuck her red cast out and pointed to a heart she had drawn under her dad's signature and above mine.

"That's a pretty heart," I said. My voice came out high-pitched and awkward.

One minute, I had been feeling up her dad's sexy body, and the next, she was declaring her dad and me in love. This kid stuff wasn't for the faint of heart—or me.

"I've got to go help the girls in there. It was good to see you, Maisy. I hope you feel so much better and have a quick recovery. Remember, don't let anyone push you around or bully you." I cupped my hand over my mouth and leaned down to whisper in her ear, "You kick them straight in those quaffle balls if they do."

She giggled and nodded her head before straightening herself up under her dad's curious gaze.

"Got it, Miss Betty! Thank you for that choco taco! And this!" She stuck out her cast again, pointing to the heart she had drawn.

I nodded at them both and ran back into the taco truck. I forced myself to not look back.

"Well?" Rox sat on the edge of the back door to the truck, swinging her feet back and forth.

"I don't know what the hell I just did. I couldn't think when he had his muscles out and in my face like that. I just ... I invited him on a trip."

"You did what?" Nikki stood behind Rox with her mouth hanging open in horror.

"It gets worse. That trip is to meet my family. My aunt got married and invited me. And my dumbass was getting all hot and bothered, looking at that chiseled jaw, and I just—shit! How am I going to get out of this?" I leaned against the back of the truck and took a deep breath.

"You're fucked," Layla said. "I've never seen you frazzled. I'm kind of scared."

"Oh, shut it." I rubbed the back of my neck and closed my eyes.

I wouldn't admit it, but I was scared too. Whatever chaos I'd been dealing with in the last two days would be nothing compared to the chaos of introducing my new boy toy to my family. And that wasn't even the scary part. The scary part was that, even knowing about the upcoming disaster, I still felt a tiny bit excited. I felt things inside me that I hadn't thought possible. When Terrance had said he liked me, I'd felt butterflies. Butterflies! I hadn't even known such a beautiful thing could live inside my dead soul. But here I was, Queen B, catching feelings over a man. If my crotchety, old aunt May could settle with a man and be happy, perhaps there was hope for me too. Not that I wanted it. Yet.

"Let's get back to work. I got money to make!" I pushed myself off the back of the truck and clapped my hands together, ignoring the silence and the curious eyes of my besties. I couldn't explain to them what was going on when I couldn't even explain it to myself.

SIX

Terrance

I drove to Betty's house in nervous excitement. I couldn't believe I'd committed to an overnight stay with her family. I barely even knew Betty, and if her family was anything like her, I was fucked. She scared me but in a way that I liked. Not only physically, but in my feels too. The way she couldn't keep her hands off of me the other day had me ravenous for her. Sure, women loved to touch my rippled abs. But Betty usually held out. But that last time I had seen her, she'd let herself go.

The second she had trailed her palm down my chest, my dick had jumped in my pants, begging for more. If I hadn't had Maisy with me, I would have grabbed her hand and taken her to my truck. It wouldn't have been the first time I screwed in the backseat of my truck. I hadn't bought an extended cab just because I needed space and a place for a car seat. Being a single dad limited my options on fuckery. I took it where I could get it. This old truck of mine had been my mobile hotel for years.

The women I'd dated didn't seem to mind. Almost all of them were more than happy to strip down and bounce on my ride—in my ride. My stamina ran like a diesel too. Slow to warm up, but once I got going, I barreled through. Unstoppable. From my experience with Betty the other day, her libido perfectly matched mine. Except I'd never been submissive before.

All the women I had ever been with weren't exactly shy about what they wanted, but they had never been ballsy enough to take it from me either. Even the ladies in the strip club liked to play like they were some type of wild animal, but when I got them alone, they just went with the flow. My flow. I set the pace, and they followed through. But with Betty, the way she'd grabbed me, using me how she wanted ... *damn*. She'd made my balls tingle, my dick twitch, and my heart flutter.

I hadn't had the heart flutters since I was with Maisy's mom. For the longest time, I'd thought she had taken those flutters with her, and I'd never see them again. I'd thought I was dead in love, and no one could awaken that side of me again. My focus remained on my daughter anyway. I didn't have the time to let myself feel flutters. The dates I'd been on in the last few years were short-lived. There were lots of one-night stands, flings, and absolutely no flutters.

But Betty ...

After getting a taste of her, my entire body had fluttered. I wasn't exactly truthful when I told her that Maisy insisted on seeing her. That part was real. But I had left out that I wanted to see her again too. I couldn't hold out. I wanted to get this thing moving along and finish what we had started. Maisy had been the perfect excuse.

A pang of dad guilt shot through me as I realized my kid was my wingman. I quickly shook that thought away, remembering what my dad had said at the hospital after Betty left.

"You'd better not let that one go," my dad said, settling back into the hospital chair. He had a smirk on his face, as if he knew an important secret and wanted to dangle it in front of my face, teasing.

"Why? We're just dating. Nothing serious." I shrugged my shoulders, avoiding eye contact with my daughter, who was staring up at me with her puppy-dog eyes. I wasn't sure what she wanted.

Bullshit. I knew. She didn't want me to let that one go either.

"Because of the way you two looked at one another. Haven't ever seen that look on you before." He kept smirking. "Not even with … you know …"

"And how was that? How did we look at each other?" I tilted my head, waiting on whatever excitement he was trying to hold back.

"Like this, Daddy! I saw it too!" Maisy said, wiggling her brows up and down her tiny forehead so fast that I thought they'd fly off.

"Okay, this convo is over. Let me find a nurse, so we can get out of here!" I turned on my heel to go, leaving Maisy's wiggling brows and my dad's roaring laughter behind me.

I fumbled with the radio, stopping on a rap station before quickly turning it to something different. I didn't want Betty to think I was stereotyping and listening to rap for her. That would be just the thing she would accuse me of doing. I had to be on high alert not to offend her.

She had already told me not to stereotype when I insisted I was the man and I'd pay for the plane tickets. That had been a feisty and quick conversation that ended with her saying, "Boy, bye," and hanging up the phone before I could argue.

She was the one who wanted to take me on this little trip, but even still, my dad had raised me to be a gentleman. Minus the stripper alter ego that shook my dick at women, I always treated the ladies top-notch, like the queens they were. Maybe I had mommy issues—scratch that. I knew I had mommy issues. I shuddered, disgusted with myself. I was a single-dad stripper with mommy issues. I had to keep my head in the game and remain focused on growing my money, so I could be a single-dad bar owner with no issues. I laughed to myself.

As if people were walking around this planet with no issues. Speaking of …

I pulled into Betty's driveway, nearly hitting her as she marched toward my truck.

"Jeez! You scared the crap out of me! Didn't know you'd be waiting outside. Hey, where's your mom?"

I hopped out of my truck and ran to help Betty with her luggage, but she shrugged me off. She had texted me earlier in the week, asking if I cared if her mother tagged along. Of course, I wanted Betty to myself, but who was I to say no to Betty's mother?

"She's not coming." Betty bit her bottom lip and avoided my gaze, throwing her overnight bag in the bed of my truck.

I heard the frustration in her voice and hoped this wasn't a bad omen of our first trip together. "Why not?"

"Because that's just how she is. Can't depend on her for shit. She's probably too busy nursing one of her deadbeat boyfriends after a binger." She climbed into my truck and buckled her seat belt.

I noticed a slight tremble in her hands before she curled them into fists and shoved them under her armpits, folding her arms like armor against her chest.

"Oh. But you bought her a ticket," I said, pulling away from her house.

I flipped my bright lights on and focused my eyes on the dark road ahead of me.

"Nonrefundable too. She doesn't care. And neither do I. This is our vacation. I'm not going to let her or anyone ruin it." Betty leaned her head back. "You know, I don't say this often, but you were right on driving. I can sleep. I guess that's one pro of giving in to you."

I laughed, thinking back on our conversation the day before.

"So, I'll pick you up at four thirtyish," I said.

"Do what?" Betty huffed so loud that I had to hold the phone away from my ear. "Why can't I drive?"

"It's only to the airport. Besides, I've seen how you drive."

"The hell does that mean?"

"You said yourself that you'd been trained by a race car driver."

"I didn't say he trained me. He screwed me. Took me for a ride. Showed me around the track. Know what I'm saying?"

A searing heat shot through my chest before quickly fading into an unsettling feeling. If whoever Race Car Jones was had taken Betty for a ride instead of her taking him for a ride, I had competition. I could never picture Betty being submissive, but the thought of her looking up at me while on her knees did set me on fire.

"You mean, you tied him up and rode his pocket rocket?" I probed, hoping I wasn't coming off too obvious.

"No. I mean, he grabbed his stick shift and took me for some laps."

"I thought you were only into being the dominant one." I lowered my voice and stepped out the back door of Scarlett Herb. I hadn't planned on taking a break, but this conversation called for privacy.

"How did we go from arguing over who was driving to talking about my sexcapades? You tell me yours. I know you've had a lot of partners. I've seen the way you move them hips. If I were blind and I felt you move on me like that, I'd think you were Black."

"Actually, I am one percent Nigerian. I did one of those DNA test things."

"Explains the dick and the dance. But you gotta work on some things. You'll figure it out once I throw you into the pit of my family."

"What things do I need to work on?" I sat down on the stoop of the cement stairs and pulled at my collar.

The leaves were beginning to change. Before too long, the holidays would be here, and a blanket of snow would cover Outer Forks. I wasn't a fan of snow, but ever since that damn Frozen movie, Maisy had become obsessed with snow. One time, when I'd left her alone for two minutes, she'd gotten into the pantry and ripped open a bag of powdered sugar. She tried to make a snowman on the dinner table by mixing water, soap, and powdered sugar. That had been three years ago, and my floors were still sticky.

"First, you need to learn to give a Black woman her way. Or else you're in trouble. Actually, all women." She laughed into the phone.

I smiled, hearing that familiar sound. No one laughed like Betty. The sound she made was enticing. She had one of those laughs that called to you across the room. People gravitated toward it, curious if it was contagious. Hopeful. Everyone needed a laugh like Betty's.

"I'm starting to see that. But—"

"Don't say but. *I hate that word. Don't you dare say* but. *Everything you say before* but *is canceled. That's the truth."*

"Okay. I won't say but. *I will say that I want to drive because I am out of the way to the airport. So, you'd be picking me up, turning around, and then heading to the airport. It doesn't make sense. Plus, let me at least do something. You bought the ticket and refused to let me pay. You're the one taking me to Memphis. I'll take you to the airport." I leaned my shoulder against the cold iron railing.*

I'd said my part, and I was too tired to argue. If she still wanted to be stubborn about it, I'd let her. I didn't have the energy to deal with it.

"All right, I agree. Makes sense. I'll see you in the morning."

"Really?" My heart lurched down into the pit of my stomach.

I'd had no idea convincing her would be that easy. I wondered what she had planned or if maybe my sexual questions had frazzled her into cutting the conversation short.

"Just this one time. But if you get us there late because you drive like a grandma, we're going to have problems."

"I promise to be on time and not drive like an old lady. I'll put my lead foot on and leave my compression socks and bunion cream at home."

"Okay, boomer. Let's see how well you stick to your word. See you tomorrow."

"See you tomorrow," I said, grinning into the phone.

I wanted to bring up the race car driver again, to prod into her personal life some more, but she'd already drifted off to sleep. Her head was leaning against the passenger window. Those luscious ruby lips of hers weren't flapping for once, but instead, they were shut in the softest of expressions. She almost looked innocent while she slept. Almost.

Her eyes flew open the second I parked my truck. We both let out tired groans as we stretched and gathered our bags before heading into the airport. Luckily, Outer Forks was dead at this hour. We moved through check-in and boarded our almost-empty flight with ease. I stuffed our luggage in the bin above us and settled into the seat beside Betty. She hadn't spoken much at all since I picked her up.

"Tired?" I asked, rubbing her shoulder.

She flinched, closing her eyes for a split second. Her chest stopped moving before she took a deep breath and spoke, "I'm sorry. I've been quiet. I know. Yes, I'm tired. But it's not physical. I have that dragging mental exhaustion that some people seem to do to me." She let out a sigh.

Anxiety rose into my throat, tightening my chest. I hoped I hadn't crossed the line by asking about the race car driver the other day. "Was it something I said?"

"No, of course not!" She reached out and rubbed my knee before twisting her body to face me. "It's not you. It's my mom. For some dumb reason, I actually hoped she was coming, that this time would be different. It doesn't matter. We're going to have a good time. You get to meet my aunt May. Or whatever her last name is these days. Can't believe she's married now!"

I tried to listen as best as I could and offer empathy for her wishy-washy mother, but the way her hand rested on my leg distracted me from any words coming out of her mouth. All I could do was stare at her parted lips and imagine the way they'd tightly wrap around my cock. Fantasizing about that bubblegum-pink tongue sliding back and forth over the tip sent my foot bouncing in anticipation. I tuned every word she said out. I couldn't help it.

"Are you okay?" She laughed, bringing me back down to reality. Her mouth grew even wider, showing me the back of her throat.

Damn, I want to blow my load back there. Watch her swallow every ounce.

"Yep. Why?" I said, continuing to stare at her mouth.

"You're breathing funny. And you can't look me in the eyes. I asked you how Maisy was doing, and you just grunted. I asked about your dad, and you grunted. I then asked you about your right big toe, and you grunted. What's up? What are you thinking about?" She pulled back in her seat and shimmied her top down, exposing the slightest hint of cleavage.

"Oh, you're a tease." I shook my head.

"I know. Just wait until we get to that hotel. I'm going to show you how much I can tease."

"I thought we were staying with your aunt or family. You got us a hotel?"

"Course I did! I can't be getting it on at my family's house. That's just nasty. Don't you know, I can't keep my mouth shut? How do you think I am in bed? Might as well hold a concert in my bedroom. I didn't get to finish the other day. I have finished at least eight times since then but not with a man. And not with Tito, my muscleman. Or Terrance, my muscleman. Whichever alter ego you're bringing tonight."

"I'll bring them both." I grinned.

The plane pulled out of the terminal and accelerated down the runway. Every small bump we glided over sent Betty's boobs bouncing. My head bounced in rhythm.

"A spit-roast. Now, you're talking." She had that wild look in her eyes again that made my asshole clench tight.

"Hold up now. I didn't say anything about adding another." I put my hand up in protest.

"I'm just messing with you. We can talk about that at a later date. You're all mine tonight." She wiggled herself into a comfortable position as we lifted off the runway.

"No deal. I'll never consider sharing you. You're not too much woman for me. I can handle you by myself, thanks," I huffed.

I mentally pictured myself and the race car driver tied up in her dungeon, both of us pining for her attention. I clamped my jaw shut, grinding my teeth.

"Puh-lease. You don't know who you're talking to, but you're about to find out." She rested her head back and closed her eyes, blowing out her breath like she'd just heard a load of bullshit. But the smile that crept over her face, the one she fought to hold back, told me otherwise. She liked what I'd said.

Little Miss Badass Betty wants me to make her mine after all...

We stepped out of the plane and into stifling heat. I'd already broken a sweat before we left the airport.

"Damn. I had no idea Memphis was this hot! It's fall! What the hell?" I stuck my tongue out, panting.

Opening the airport doors to the outside felt like opening the gates of hell. A blast of heat struck me so hard across my cheeks that I was sure Memphis was really Satan's oven. That was fitting, seeing that Betty was from here. I thought I'd tease her a bit about it, but the look on her face told me she wasn't in the mood.

"If you can't handle the heat, better get outta the kitchen! Besides, it's the Dirty South. We don't have that fresh mountain air here like we do back home. What do you expect? This is my hometown. They don't call it the city of Grit and Grind for nothing. The only reason I haven't moved back is because there's no way I'm leaving DTF."

"Why did you move away from it then?" I asked, slowly trailing behind her.

I waded through the heat like I was swimming in molasses. I'd always considered Outer Forks a part of the South, but we had the luxury of higher elevation, which meant non-swamp-like heat in our summers.

"My mom and her twin sister moved to Outer Forks together when I was younger. Then, they had some drama and split. Probably why she isn't coming. She thinks her evil twin sister will show up at Aunt May's. Anyway, I was little. I don't remember much of Memphis, except for when I came here to visit family. It's my type of place though. You'll see soon enough."

"I'm not sure I could handle the heat, but if you say so. Where to? I'll get an Uber." I pulled my phone out of my sweaty-ass pocket, noticing the couple next to us scoffing.

In Outer Forks, no one batted an eye, seeing Betty and me together. But I had already seen a few vicious glances toward us in the airport. I pretended not to notice. I didn't want to upset Betty, but I was sure she had seen them too.

"Central Station. And thanks. For once, we aren't going to fight over who drives." She walked a few steps down from the couple, set her bag on the sidewalk, and plopped herself beside it.

"Time to get back up. He's already here," I said, showing her the screen before pulling her back up to her feet.

"This is going to be a long day, Terrance. But let's try to have some fun. You hungry? Maybe he'll swing by somewhere and get us food. I could use a slab of ribs and a cold beer."

"It's nine in the morning!" I laughed, reaching my arm around her and pulling her into me.

Her body softened at my touch, quite the opposite of what mine was doing. One caress of her shoulder, and my dick throbbed. I moved my overnight bag in front of the bulge growing in my pants.

"And? You know you're going to have to stay intoxicated to put up with my family. Better stop by the liquor store anyway. Can't show up empty-handed." She sighed, fanning herself.

"Wait. Isn't this a wedding party? No bartender there?" I leaned back, searching her eyes.

"This is a get-together after the wedding. Not a formal event. Lawdy, Terrance. It's not being catered by Scarlett Herb mixologists." She winked.

"Okay. Got it. Bring liquor. Check."

I kissed her forehead. I wasn't sure why I had done that. It just happened. I didn't crave a kiss on the lips, though I'd take that too. I'd dive-bombed straight into her forehead, where those fluttering butterflies in my stomach had whispered for me to touch.

"What are you doing?" She squinted up at me. Her hand reached up, trailing my scruffy jawline.

"Kissing you?" I asked.

I cupped her chin in my hand and ran the pad of my thumb over that bottom lip of hers. She snarled before taking my thumb between her teeth and nibbling hard.

"Tell the driver we're going straight to the hotel. We can eat later," she growled as the Uber pulled up in front of us.

She had that wild look in her eyes again. The expression that scared me senseless yet made me want to fall on my knees and beg to taste her.

"Terrance?" the driver called through his rolled-down window.

"That's us. Central Station!" I replied, shuffling into the backseat.

Betty scooted in beside me. She rubbed her body right up against mine, practically pushing me into the car door. Smothered again but this time by her entire body in the backseat of an Uber ride. I thought back to her sex dungeon and the way she'd smothered me with that sweet pussy of hers. I couldn't breathe then, and I couldn't breathe now. The Memphis heat, coupled with ferocious Betty, was a match that I couldn't withstand. Maybe she was right. Perhaps I couldn't handle her.

I began to panic that I wouldn't be enough man for her. I had the sense that she wanted me to try at least, but how far was too far with a woman like her? I wondered if I'd offend her if I played boss in bed. She rested her hand on my thigh and side-eyed me while discreetly moving it closer and closer to my dick.

I laid my head back and closed my eyes, pretending to sleep—for the driver. The lower half of my body remained wide awake and playful. The closer Betty's hand inched toward my johnson, the more I thrust my hips in the air against it. Enough of this *dancing around each other* bullshit. As soon as we checked into the hotel, all bets were off. I couldn't stand to wait for her to bring all her bells and whistles out and make me beg for it. I needed her now.

I pressed my lips together and sucked in my breath through my nose. With each deep breath I stifled, I felt myself become more and more rigid. Wild. Primal. Betty must have felt it, too, because, by now, her hand was gripping my cock so tight that she might as well have been strangling it. Good. I didn't plan to be gentle with her either.

The driver bobbed his head to the music, singing along, while Betty felt me up in the backseat. If he looked in the rearview mirror, all he would see was two sleepy passengers. If he turned his head toward us in the back, he'd see her fistful of cock. I bit my lip in an anxious fit. Blood pumped through my veins in tune to the beat of whatever hard rock our driver was playing, which in turn, beat to the rhythm of Betty's squeezes.

My heart pounded against my chest as I situated myself, putting my arm around her so I could lean down and whisper into her ear. "I'm going to touch your hair," were the words that flowed out of my mouth. Yep. Total douche bag, right? I could have told her how I wanted to slip my cock down her throat or bend her over and smack that ass of hers, but nope. Instead, I could only think of one thing to get her riled up and know I meant business—her hair.

"The fuck you say?" She shot back in her seat, removing her hand from my cock as if she'd burned it on a hot stove.

Now was my chance. I could cower down to her and whimper an apology, or I could stick it through and dish her ferocity back at her times two. Or at least times one and a half. I hoped. My eyes flashed toward the driver before staring straight back into hers.

"I'm going to wrap those curls around my fist. Winding it up around my wrist so that I can pull your neck back, exposing it to my teeth, while I push myself deep inside of you. That's what I'm going to do. Is there a problem?" I snarled, staring at her chest instead of meeting her gaze.

I hoped she couldn't read my eyes. I didn't have a poker face. Right now, I was pretty sure all I wore was a *please don't hurt me and just let me fuck you* face.

I refused to look at her , so I couldn't see if I'd shocked her or excited her. But the second I felt her warm breath tickle my ear, I knew I'd scored.

"That's a big step, you know. No one touches my hair. But I'll let you. It'd damn well better be worth it." She bit my ear hard, causing me to yelp.

We stayed close together, breathing heavily and caressing each other until we pulled up to Central Station. By now, I could feel myself dripping. I ached with the need to feel her and fill her. We tumbled out of the car, waved good-bye to the driver, and checked in at the hotel as quickly as possible.

"I booked an early check-in. Under Betty Willis." Betty tapped her foot against the concrete floor. Her heels clacked like a whip cutting through the air, drowning out the faint bluesy tunes drifting throughout the lobby.

"This is the train station. It's still new. The hotel is, I mean. Pretty badass, isn't it?" She cocked her head toward a wall of retro speakers stretching alongside the back of the entrance. "There's a bar downstairs that serves up your type of craft cocktails. They usually have someone spinning records in the evening too." She looked me up and down, smiling. "Told you, Memphis is awesome. Welcome to the Dirty South, Terrance. Or dirtier south than Outer Forks anyway."

I grinned, sinking into the comfortable vibe surrounding us. The music beat softly, and the guests milled about, laughing. The faint scent of barbecue intoxicated me into a trance I'd never felt before.

"This is pretty awesome. But you know what?" I picked up our bags as soon as the receptionist handed her the room keys. My biceps strained under the weight of whatever Betty had packed for one night. I assumed it was half of her sex dungeon.

"What?" she asked, reaching out to touch my arm. Her fingertips brushed against my muscles, making them twitch.

"You're way more awesome. And you're going to look awesome as I slam into you from behind. Give me that key." I snatched the key from her hand, grabbed her elbow, and led her to our room.

I grinned, detecting a bounce in her step as her heels echoed down the hall.

"I'm going to let you take control. But don't get any ideas. I don't do this often. I—"

I smashed my lips into hers, pushing her up against our hotel room door. I pulled her bottom lip between my teeth, sucking hard enough to make her gasp.

"Don't talk," I said, unlocking the door and throwing the luggage on the floor.

"Excuse me? What do you mean? I can't say—"

"Shh." I put my hand over her mouth.

She growled out from under it but kept her mouth closed. I walked her backward to the bed, our steps in sync, rushing, needing, aching. I gathered her shirt in my fists and pulled it over her head. She flinched as I tugged it over her hair. I unbuckled my belt and let my pants drop to the floor.

"Boy, you'd better watch it. And I hope you have a rubber for your miniature."

"Miniature? Do what? You think my dick's small?" My hands fell from her breasts to my sides.

"No! That's what I call it—your miniature. You know, like a mini me. Ugh. Just keep going. Wrap that shit up though." She slipped her palm under the waistline of my pants and pulled me toward her.

"I'm fucking this pig. You're just holding the tail." I turned her around and bent her over the side of the bed.

"What did you just call me?"

She looked back at me, gripping my cock as if, this time, she really was going to strangle it until it fell off. I could see it turning purple already.

"It's an expression! You know, it means, I'm in control. Not that you're a pig. Or not that I fuck pigs. Shit! Just … forget it. We can't dirty-talk, I guess. We'll have to work on that." I groaned.

She rolled her eyes before unbuttoning her pants and shimmying out of them. "Show me what you got, Mr. Terrance." She slipped out of her panties while staring at me with the most innocent look I'd ever seen on her.

There's that juicy ass I've been waiting to make mine.

I tightened my jaw and fished my wallet out of my back pocket, quickly rolling a condom over my *miniature.*

Her hands spread out before her, smoothing over the white sheets as she arched her back, sticking her ass up in the air impatiently. I licked my fingertips and dived them straight into her, watching the way she clawed at the sheets gathering in her fists.

"Like I said, you're mine." I reached up toward her hair, and as gentle as I could at the moment, I began wrapping her curls around my wrist.

She let out a moan, took a deep breath, and looked back at me, wide-eyed. I tugged hard, yanking her neck back and crawling above her. Her back flexed, tempting me into biting her shoulder before I guided myself into her.

"Oh, damn." Her thighs shook as soon as I slipped inside her wet pussy.

She was soaked. I'd only taken a few strokes, and already, she began dripping down my balls.

"Fuck," I breathed out, relaxing so much that I almost fell over.

"Do it. Give it to me. You'd better bring it. Else I'm going to reach back and flip you over me and climb on top!" she ordered, growling back at me.

I pushed her with my hips down into the bed harder. I couldn't sit back and savor this round. I needed to drill into her like I knew she'd drill into me.

I let go of her hair and grabbed her wrists, pinning them behind her back as I slammed into her. Her voice rang out, bouncing off the walls. I didn't care. The louder she screamed, the rougher I became. My heart rate quickened as I watched her struggle. She bucked her hips back against mine, screaming for more. I kept going, but at this rate, I didn't know who was fucking who anymore.

We fought against each other in a fit of growls and moans. Her ass pushed back hard on my hips while my hands grabbed hers and kept them pinned against her lower back.

She buried her head into the bed and yelled, "Come for me, baby. I need to feel you throb inside of me. Do it, Tito! Terrance! Now!"

I hadn't known I was close to coming, but the second she gave the order, it sent me straight over the edge. As much as I loved taking control, I much preferred Betty as a boss lady. I had to make too many decisions and overthink my busy life already. Betty taking over and giving me commands was a sweet and sexy relief.

I squeezed her hands together, strangling them until her fingertips began to turn pink. My legs shook out from under me, causing me to lean down above her. I couldn't stand it any longer. I twisted her arms above her head and quivered. She leaned her head back, looking up at me and giving me that wide, devilish grin. I tried to smile, but smiling while having an explosive orgasm wasn't easy. I was sure I looked like I was constipated. That was not the message I wanted to send.

What is the message I want to send? Oh, yeah, she's mine. I got this.

"I love you!" I screamed as I spilled out inside her.

Shit! No, that wasn't the message.

DEAD.

That devilish grin of hers collapsed into a horrified terror. I awkwardly slowed my pace before stopping and pulling out. Neither one of us said anything. She wasn't even breathing.

"Uh, I'm going to go clean up," I said, breaking the silence and running off to the bathroom.

I locked myself inside and peeled off the condom, throwing it in the trash before sitting my bare ass down on the cold lid of the toilet. I didn't hear a peep from the other room and wondered if I had killed Betty with shock. I felt that way myself.

I tried to make sense of those idiotic three words I'd blurted out during the throes of passion. I wanted to tell myself it was just an *in the moment* feelings thing. But the more I sat on the toilet, thinking about it, the more I realized I was lying to myself. I did love Betty.

I stood up and splashed cold water on my face, hoping to wake up and clear my mind before I had to face her again. I needed to tell her that I really was falling in love with her. But I couldn't do that just yet. Not now. If she didn't say it back, the trip would be ruined. And if I knew anything about Betty, she was guarded like a fort. Fort Betty. Getting into her would require more than fucking her senseless.

Though she did let me touch her hair. That is serious business, I mused.

"You can't hide forever, lover boy," she called from the room.

I grinned, tilting my chin up and checking my reflection in the mirror. I couldn't stall the inevitable.

SEVEN

Betty

I told the driver to stop by a liquor store before we made our way to my aunt May's house. Terrance insisted on bringing a couple of things so that he could make a few drinks for the newlyweds. He purchased two bags full of liquor, plastic cups, and even had the Uber driver stop at the grocery store for garnishments. I had no idea what he planned, but I insisted that he let me handle everything and ease him into the party before he played Mr. Show-Off.

"I'm not showing off. I'm a mixologist. I'm offering my skills and booze! I can't show up empty-handed to a party anyway. That would be offensive. It's not like I can bring a casserole. Can I? Think we can pick up something? What kind of food is there?" Terrance asked.

"Terrance, Terrance, Terrance. You ain't ever been to a Black party? No one picks something up. They make it all. Patrice makes the potatoes. Aunt May makes the roast and her crack cookies. My mom usually brings the macaroni and cheese …" My voice trailed off at the mere mention of my mother.

I couldn't say I was shocked that she hadn't come. She'd done this several times, and each time, I'd thought she'd be different. I'd thought she'd actually follow through with her plans and want to spend some time with me. But nope. That never happened. Every time I reached out to her, I got burned, and yet I never learned my lesson.

"I can cook a mean spinach-artichoke dip, but I don't have a kitchen." He crossed his arms and tapped his chin.

I could practically see the gears turning in his head. He had worn the same expression when he tried to excuse his love confession post-orgasm.

He'd apologized when he came out of the bathroom. He'd said, sometimes, he would say things in the heat of the moment that he didn't mean. I'd already known it was bullshit. He couldn't love me. We'd known each other for months but not gotten to know one another yet. This little vacation to meet my family would be a test in his patience. Inevitably, after he saw where I'd come from, he'd run for the hills. And if I was honest with myself, maybe that was why I'd invited him.

Because truth be told, I liked Terrance too. The way my body lit up when he was nearby had scared me into pushing him away. Hence, taking him to my aunt May's house. He would see the craziness of my crew and nope the fuck out for his and Maisy's sake. The timing for him in need of a vacation and me in need of a reality check had matched up perfectly.

"You aren't going to bring spinach-artichoke dip to my family's house. I doubt they even know what an artichoke is. Now, if you'd said some nachos or something, we could work with that. But it's okay. Really. The booze is enough. I already got her a card and some cash as a gift. It doesn't get better than that. We're good." I pulled my pocket mirror out of my handbag and smoothed my hair down. It wasn't on the level I had wanted it to be when my family saw me, but then again, Terrance pulling it had been worth it.

"Your hair looks beautiful. Quit fussing with it. I'm sorry if I messed it up, but it looks amazing to me." He put his arm around me and pulled me closer.

He'd spritzed himself with cologne before we left. That scent on him brought out my inner ho.

"You can mess it up again. Later," I growled into his ear as we pulled up to my aunt's house.

Already, there were cars lined up and down the street. I could hear the crowd and smell the food before we exited the Uber. Finally, I felt at home. I thanked the driver and hopped out of the backseat, pulling Terrance with me.

"Quick rundown," I said, gathering the bags of liquor.

"I know; I know. Don't talk. Let you handle everything until everyone has had at least one or two drinks. Then, I can open my White-boy mouth."

He grabbed the paper bag from my hands with his fists, flexing his biceps. If I could marry anything, it would be those biceps. His muscles were as big as my head, and I didn't have the smallest head. Especially with my hair done up like it was supposed to look like today anyway. I reached up, smoothing it down again.

"Why do you gotta say it like that? No one said anything about your White-boy mouth. All I'm saying is, just let me handle my family and slowly introduce you into the situation."

A group of young kids ran from the backyard, screaming and laughing before disappearing again around the house. I reached into the liquor bag and grabbed a small bottle of my favorite whiskey, quickly stashing it into my purse.

"There's a situation?" He gulped, clutching the bags to his chest.

"Not if you follow my lead. I've never even bought a man over here. Let alone a White one. We're a very prideful family. I don't know how this is going to go. But I think we'll be all right." I slowly dragged my feet toward the back gate. I wasn't a nervous person, but introducing Terrance to my family was the dumbest idea I'd ever had. And I wasn't new to dumbass ideas.

What was I thinking?

"Look what the cat dragged in! And she brought white bread!" My cousin LaJuana laughed, hopping up from her favorite spot on top of the blue cooler and rushing to be the first to greet us.

"Don't even start. LaJuana, this is Terrance. Terrance, this is my cousin LaJuana." I cleared my throat, skimming the rest of the guests for my aunt May.

"At least he has a Black name. What else does he have in common with my Black brothers?" LaJuana smirked, staring at Terrance's crotch before flicking her eyes to his.

"I'd shake your hand, but ..." Terrance held up the bags of liquor.

"Go on, get! You're a mess," Aunt May said, shooing LaJuana back. "I'm so glad you made it. Where's your mom? And who is this?" She raised her eyebrows before pulling me into a hug.

I shook my head and shrugged, unable to make excuses for my mother.

"No worries. We both know how that goes." She rubbed my back.

Terrance had run to the cooler to drop off the liquor and quickly jogged back to offer his hand to Aunt May and congratulate her.

"He's my"—I hesitated—"friend. Terrance is my friend."

"Well, come on, friend. Let me introduce you to everyone else. Might as well get the hard part over with. Thanks for the booze too." Aunt May tugged at Terrance's shirt, slowly running her palm up to his bicep first. She shivered.

"I can make you a drink first, if you'd like. I might need one myself." Terrance bit his lip, avoiding the gaze of every other guest.

Even the music pumping through the yard couldn't drown out the awkward silence that had fallen on the party as soon as we arrived.

"Oh. My. Gosh. Another White man. And did I just hear you say you'd make our drinks? Marilyn May, introduce me. John should be around here somewhere. He needs to see this man too. Phew, Lord. You must be Betty," said a man I'd never seen before. "I'm Grayson. Your aunt is the coolest old person ever. John! Come here, please!" he yelled across the yard, motioning to another man.

Both John and Grayson looked like they'd stepped out of an action movie. They wore their hair slicked back, and their muscles would give my man's—I meant, Terrance's—some competition.

"Here we go. If you ever call me an old person again, I will bake you in a casserole, Grayson." Aunt May rolled her eyes.

"Ahh, I see where you get it from now." Terrance nodded.

I raised my brows at him, unsure if this turn of events and his playful teasing was a good or bad thing.

"These men don't learn, do they?" Aunt May said while John, Grayson, and Terrance chatted. "But I found one that does. Kind of. He's good to me anyway. Come meet Clyde. Let the White boys have their moment." Aunt May whisked me away while Grayson and John tugged Terrance toward the liquor table.

I followed Aunt May inside, passing familiar faces and the curious eyes of people I'd yet to meet. Every once in a while, I'd stop to give an uncle or cousin a hug or fist bump. I stepped over a group of kids playing Spades.

"Teach 'em young, ain't that right?" a man said, putting his arm around Aunt May.

"Betty, this is Clyde. Clyde, this is my niece I told you about, Betty." Aunt May beamed up at Clyde. Beamed!

Just what the hell is going on here?

I'd never seen my aunt this happy before. She usually wore a scowl and wanted to round all the men up and send them down the river. But the look she was giving Clyde unsettled me into needing one of Terrance's drinks, stat.

"Nice to meet you, Clyde. How you won over this feisty lady is beyond me. But you two look happy. Congratulations." I shook his hand.

"Thank you. I don't know how I won her over either, but damn, I'm glad I did. She's one hell of a woman." Clyde pulled Aunt May in tighter.

"So, how did you meet? Old folks' home? Bingo night? At the doctor's office?" I smirked, teasing my not-so-easily offended Aunt.

"Child, please. We met on Tinder. Though there was a bingo night in there." Aunt May brushed her shoulder off and raised her eyebrows at me.

"Are you kidding me? Tinder?" I laughed loud enough to draw the attention of my sister, Patrice, and nieces, who barged through the door.

"Kids, go to Aunt Betty. I am D-O-N-E!" Patrice threw her hands in the air before heading over to us.

We went through introductions again while my nieces waited impatiently for my attention. All five of them hopped up and down on their feet, asking me if I'd brought them anything. Typically, I gave them small gifts when I saw them, which was often enough. They only lived about two hours or so from me. But I'd had no idea they were traveling to Memphis this weekend. My sister was a single mom, and her work schedule usually took over her weekends.

"I don't have anything today. Sorry! I didn't know I'd be seeing y'all. But if you steal me some of those crack cookies of Aunt May's, I'll play a round of Spades with you, and the winner gets a twenty. How does that sound?" I asked, shouting out after them as they ran away to grab cookies.

"Thanks," Patrice sighed. "I just need a moment. That's all. Are you alone?"

"I understand. And nope, I'm not. I … brought a man," I muttered.

Patrice sucked in her breath. "Judas Priest! Traitor! I thought we didn't get attached. Where is my partner in crime?"

"Who said I'm getting attached? Besides, look at Aunt May. She is the true villain. She got married, for goodness' sake!"

We turned our attention to the happy couple and both gagged.

"Introduce me later. I'm going to get a drink. I need it after that flight. I'm guessing Mom isn't coming? I didn't even talk to her. I just … can't right now."

"No. She didn't come. Same shit, different day." I fished the whiskey out of my purse, took a sip, and passed it to my sister.

"Thanks. Bottoms up." She took a swig before handing the bottle back to me and shuffling off toward the backyard.

I turned, greeting the people around me. Some of my family I hadn't seen in years. Others I didn't care to see for years to come. Still, family was family, and I was happy for Aunt May and Clyde.

I plopped myself on the floor, feeling the heat of the whiskey hit my belly. My nieces came running back to me. The eldest, Kali, handed me a plate of cookies and sat down beside me, pulling a deck of cards out of her training bra. She reminded me of myself a bit too much. I prayed she wouldn't be as wild as me when she hit those teenage years, which would be too soon for my sister's liking.

"Thanks, Kali. Let's start. I don't have too long. I've got company with me. But we can do a quick game."

"That's because you have a boyfriend here, and you'd rather be cuddling up next to him than be with your own blood." Kali crossed her arms over her chest and bobbed her head side to side.

"Yep. Now, deal 'em." I nodded toward the cards, grabbed a cookie, and snuck another swig of whiskey.

I sat on the floor of the tiny living room, playing cards with my nieces for damn near an hour before I saw Terrance again. He headed toward me with two plates piled high with food.

"Sorry. I tried to get back earlier, but I met your sister, Patrice, and she said she'd cut me if I took her babysitter away. I told her I understood the need for a break. But it has been over an hour, and I figured you might need one too." he said, handing me a plate. "Be right back!" He ran off and returned with two drinks before sitting cross-legged beside me.

I shooed my nieces away to eat and give me some space.

"Mmhmm. So? You ready to head back to Outer Forks yet?" I asked Terrance, slowly sipping my drink. Whatever he'd made tasted like sweet nectar of the gods on my lips. Salty, sweet, and with a punch that would hit me as soon as I got up off this floor.

"What? Hell no! I'm having a blast. Even LaJuana helped me with the cocktails. I think she has mixology in her future." He grinned, digging into the plate of food. "Good God! This is divine! I'll have to tell Jay about this!" He took another bite of the roast.

"The only thing LaJuana has in her future is a pack of menthols and liver disease. Maybe Plan B too. Nice to see you were getting cozy with her though." I took another sip of my drink and shifted my eyes away.

"Wait. Are you getting jealous?" The corner of Terrance's mouth twitched up into a grin that he couldn't fight back.

"I don't get jealous," I lied, pushing the food around on my plate.

"Ah, okay. Queen B doesn't get jealous because she knows she's mine." He nodded, finishing the food on his plate and reaching for mine.

I jerked it away. "What did you say? I'm yours? Ha! Boy, bye. I'm nobody's." I rolled my eyes and tore my teeth into a roll.

"Sure, sure. Not what you were saying back at the hotel." His voice slurred.

I set my roll down on my plate. "Let's get something straight. I let you think that. But you're so damn bad right now. When we get back to that room, that ass is *mine*. M-I-N-E. You don't even know what ya got coming to you. It'll be my turn now," I snarled. My top lip curled, baring my teeth in what I hoped was a turn-on, but in reality, I probably looked like a rabid goose. I, too, felt the alcohol.

"Is that so? I'm not scared." He blew out a breath and averted his gaze.

I watched the muscle in his jaw clench tight, and his chest rose and fell quicker and quicker. My breathing sped up, matching his. We would fight this out in bed.

"Watch me," I said, grabbing him by the hand and jerking us both to our feet.

The music from the backyard thumped through the house, echoing off the walls and sending my pulse into overdrive. I pulled Terrance outside to the makeshift dirt dance floor. Somehow, the party had grown while we sat and ate. The heat of Memphis, coupled with the stifling heat of drunk-ass people, almost strangled me. But I had a point to prove. I just wasn't sure what it was.

"This is getting pretty wild," Terrance shouted at me over the music.

"My family knows how to throw a party!" I shouted back, finding LaJuana and positioning myself and Terrance right in front of her.

Of course, she was still at the liquor table, shaking her ass in a drunken chicken-headed wobble.

I closed my eyes, feeling the beat, as Terrance began to rub his hips against me. I swayed my body back and forth before bending over and pushing my ass into him, twerking it like I was trying to start a fire on his crotch. I hoped I did. I blew a kiss to LaJuana before planting my palms on the dirt and popping my ass up and into Terrance. I had never been a twerker, but Nikki had taught the whole DTF gang how to dribble our buns like we were playing ball. She had sworn that move worked to mesmerize men, and so far, she was right.

I felt Terrance's hands reach my hips and grip them tightly, pulling me into him. I stood up, turned myself toward him, and unbuttoned his shirt. If LaJuana wanted my man, too fucking bad. He was mine.

"What are you doing?" he asked, glancing around at the other dancers, who were paying us no attention.

Only LaJuana was paying attention to our show.

"Showing off my stripper boyfriend. What's it look like?" I ran my hands through his hair and down his scruffy jawline.

"Did you just say, boyfriend?" He shook his hips the same way he did onstage.

I knew if he were wearing his usual banana hammock, I'd see his juicy dick flopping all around like a helicopter coming in for a landing.

"Shush your mouth and keep dancing." I laughed, throwing my arms around his neck.

I kissed him under his ear, tasting the sweat on his skin. He tasted salty and full of alcohol, like my own personal margarita.

The music never slowed. I needed a breather, but my stripper man kept going. I stepped back to admire him, bumping into Aunt May, who had changed into the most ratchet clothes I'd seen her wear.

"What the …" I asked, sobering up at the sight of her leather getup.

"Marry him," she said, nodding to Terrance.

"You are senile or drunk." I shook my head.

Terrance kept dancing in front of us, smiling and tugging at his shirt.

Oh Lawd. Here comes Tito.

"I'm neither. Okay, that's a lie. I'm a little drunk. But I ain't senile. Look, I was wrong. Not all men are going to leave you. You know as well as I do how women are capable of that too. It's a human thing. But when you find a good one, you hang on to him. Otherwise, he's going to get snatched up."

"Clyde has brainwashed you." I dug my heels into the ground.

Grayson and John joined Terrance on the dance floor along with the White couple my aunt had introduced me to earlier—Klara and Chris. I had a feeling they were trying to pick up on his dance moves, which were, for lack of better words, not White at all.

"No, honey, he hasn't. I'm happy, and I'm in love. And I'm telling you, before you make the same mistakes I did and become bitter and shut out, take that man. Love that man. Marry that man. I see how he looks at you and, more importantly, how you look at him." She turned her head toward me, staring into my eyes, which were staring straight back at Terrance.

Mixmaster Tito had come out, and he was doing the worm on the dirt, kicking up dust all over the place. The crowd loved it, gathering around him and cheering.

"I guess so. You don't think anything of him being White, do you? I don't want to downplay my Black-girl magic or whatever. I want everyone to be okay with it." I smiled, still transfixed on Terrance and his moves.

"I don't give a damn if that boy is purple. If you're okay with it, I'm okay with it. Don't ever downplay your Black-girl magic. I have a feeling he can handle it." Aunt May put her arm around my shoulders and squeezed.

I rarely had hugs from her. This new persona was creeping me out yet also making me feel comfortable.

"Yeah, well, he did say he took one of those DNA tests and had one percent Black in him." I laughed as Terrance undid his belt and spanked it on his ass in a routine I'd seen a dozen times. I'd never tire of it.

"Oh no, honey. He has a little bit more than one percent." Aunt May shook her head and danced away toward her husband on the dance floor.

Out of the corner of my eye, I caught LaJuana starting to shimmy closer to Terrance.

Nope.

I booty-popped next to my man and whispered in his ear, "Let's go back to the hotel. I owe you one." I took the belt from his hand and smacked his ass hard.

He swooped me off my feet, kissing me square on the lips in front of LaJuana and everyone else before setting me back on the ground and grabbing my ass tight.

"Let's go," he growled.

I smirked at LaJuana, who rolled her eyes back at me, before Terrance and I disappeared out of the crowd.

He ordered the Uber while I made my rounds, bidding my family good-bye. I kissed my nieces, telling them to split the money I'd slipped them. I said good-bye to my sister and the various people I'd met whose names I'd already forgotten. Lastly, I snuck back to the dance floor to kiss my aunt good-bye.

"I'm happy for you. I love you. Come see me sometime." I held her tight. Her leather outfit stuck to my skin.

"Baby girl, my days are numbered. I'm already one foot in the grave. Do you think I'm young enough to hop on a plane and come out there? You can come to me anytime too." Aunt May kissed my forehead and held me at arm's length, looking into my eyes. "You are the spitting image of your mother. Don't let her get to you. And most of all, remember what I said. If I could go back and do it all over again, I wouldn't spend so many years alone. Go love that boy. Tonight and always."

"And what if he turns out to be a no-good piece of douche?" I asked.

I hadn't even left yet, and I already missed home. Aunt May was the mother I never had. I didn't want to go.

"Then, you say, *Thank you, next.*"

I nodded, waved good-bye, and refused to let myself cry. I bit my tongue, pressed my lips together, and rolled my eyes into the back of my head. But I did not cry. Instead, I took my man back to the hotel and fucked him senseless.

EIGHT

Terrance

"Thank you for everything. Your family was amazing. Memphis was amazing. You were and are amazing," I said, tucking back an unruly curl from Betty's face.

She not only let me touch her hair now, but she also even leaned into it.

"I'm glad you got a little break. Now, you can go back to dad life, feeling refreshed." She put her hand on my truck handle, easing the door open. "Think of a business plan for that bar of yours you want. You'll make it."

After mind-blowing sex up against the window at the hotel last night, I'd confessed all my hopes and dreams to her. We lay in bed until three a.m., talking about our past, our present, and our future. Maybe it was the mix of alcohol and the gritty city atmosphere that had made me stupid, but I'd felt like opening up to her like I'd not opened up to anyone before.

"I've worked my ass off to get to where I am. I won't ever live in poverty again. I refuse to ever feel that gnawing hunger pain. Do you

have any idea how many days I went to school without eating? If it wasn't for my aunt May—not my mom—sending me money now and then, I don't know what I'd have done. It's not like I used that money on fun stuff, like magazines and lipstick. I had to buy tampons for both my sister and me. I got our groceries at the dollar store, and even that was rough. Plus, I took care of my mom.

"But you know what I didn't do? Take care of her men that she had coming and going. One time, I was frying up some bologna, and one of them assholes reached out to grab it. I backhanded him." She sat up on one elbow, her face glowing with the reflection of the neon lights through the hotel window. The same window I'd just pushed her up against before making love to her.

I stretched my neck, glancing at our palm prints smeared against the glass. I had known she was wild, but tonight was the wildest I'd ever been. We hadn't cared if anyone saw us. Somewhere, someone was probably uploading a Betty and Terrance sex video.

"No way. Not Queen B. You're too sweet to do something like that." I laughed, running my palm down her shoulder. Her skin felt like butter.

"I did. And he didn't say a word. Just backed up and left. I never saw him again. But Mom had another loser days later. I know I'm making my mom out to be terrible. She wasn't. She went through phases where she tried to be a good mom. Making peanut butter and jelly sandwiches, buying us new shoes, or taking us to the park down the street. But those phases didn't last. She always got sucked into relationships with men who didn't deserve her. They dragged her down to her level. So, I was basically the woman of the house."

"I'm so sorry. I can't imagine the responsibility you had at a young age. I can't relate to living in poverty. But I didn't have much, and my mom was also not present. She ran away and left me with my dad before I could even remember it. A single dad raised me, and I guess I followed in his footsteps. I didn't get to go to college or do a lot of the things the other kids did, like sports. We couldn't afford those things. But I didn't go hungry.

"Still, I try to give Maisy everything I didn't have. That's why I'm working two jobs. Hopefully, one day, I can open my own bar, things will slow down, and she will understand why her daddy worked so hard. It's just tough at this age. She doesn't understand. All she understands is that Daddy is busy."

"I see. You're pulled in a lot of directions, but I think you'll get your bar. You have the focus and the drive. Maybe not the energy. I might be able to help with that. As I said, it takes a village. Plus, I like Maisy."

"What are you saying?" I sat up on my elbow, my face inches from hers.

"That I can give you a break sometimes. Let me take her to the park or something. Lord knows I know what it feels like not to have a mom. Not saying I'm going to be a mother to her." She shook her head fast. "I'm saying, I can help. But when you open that bar, you'd better heavy-hand those drinks again, and this time, they'd better be free."

I laughed, playfully bopping her nose with my fingertip before lying back down. She smiled, nestling in my arms and resting her head on my chest. We lay in a sweaty heap, tangled in the crisp sheets. The speaker in the room crooned out bluesy tunes, lulling me off to dreamland.

"I can't have people coming and going out of Maisy's life. I worry about that. Her getting her heart broken."

And me too, I thought.

"I understand that too. I'm not going to hurt that little girl." She yawned.

Or me?

I pulled her into me tighter.

"Betty?"

"Hmm?" she moaned.

Her breathing slowed and steadied. I knew she was almost asleep, but I had to know.

"What do you want? I told you what I want. My dream. But what about you? You only told me you don't want to live in poverty again. What do you want in your future?"

Her shoulder tensed under my fingertips.

"I don't know. I just really don't know."

She let out a breath, squeezing her arm around my chest. I felt her heartbeat quicken against my side. I didn't respond because I didn't *know what to say. All I could do was kiss her forehead and let myself enjoy the moment.*

"Think I can get a kiss first before you go?" I reached out, grabbing her arm and pulling her to me.

She pushed her soft lips into mine and sighed. "Keep kissing me like that, and I'm not going to get outta this truck."

"Good," I said, leaning into her and biting her lip.

"Terrance! As much as I want a quickie, I want you to get your little girl more. She's waiting for you! I don't want to be the bad guy, and she thinks that I'm keeping you from her. It can't start like that." She bobbed her head, bouncing her curls into her face.

"What's that mean, start out like that? What are we starting?" I smirked, brushing the hair from her face and nibbling her bottom lip.

She still tasted like the coffee we'd bought in the airport when we loaded up on extra caffeine. I wanted to lick her and see just how high she could get me. The blood pulsing through my veins wasn't from the espresso. Only Betty could make me feel how I felt, which was like the luckiest man alive.

"Don't start. You know what I mean." She grabbed her bag and scooted out the truck door, slamming it shut behind her.

"No, I don't. But you can explain it next time. I'll call ya. I want to see that sweet ass of yours again. And again. And maybe again," I called out.

She walked toward her front door and lifted her skirt up, showing me her ass and laughing.

"That's one out of what? Three you said? Let's see how well you behave before you get the next one," she yelled back before opening her front door and disappearing inside.

I shut my speakers off and rode in silence as I thought back on our conversations from the night before. The way she had sighed and told me she didn't know what she wanted made me slightly uneasy. If she became involved with Maisy and me and decided it wasn't what she wanted, she'd be a flight risk, which is precisely what I'd said I didn't want.

I gripped my steering wheel, going over possible scenarios of our relationship in my head. There was no doubt about it. When I'd told her I loved her, I'd meant it. I wouldn't tell her that because it was far too soon, and that would definitely make her a flight risk. But no one in my life had ever asked about my hopes and dreams. I'd never talked to a woman for hours all night. No one had sparked a light in me or held my attention.

Sure, I'd had great girlfriends and great sex. But nothing compared to Betty. She understood me, and I was pretty sure I understood her too. But I was a package deal, and given that Betty was unsure of what she wanted, I was taking a risk, even entertaining the idea that she might fall in love with me too.

I let out a loud groan and turned my music back up, giving up on love for the moment. I had the leading lady in my life waiting on me at my dad's place.

The week after my Memphis trip flashed by in a blur.

I'd only seen Betty once, Thursday, and that was when she parked The Pink Taco Truck outside of Scarlett Herb earlier in the evening. Both of us were too busy to sneak away for nooky, but she did let me feel her up behind the truck when no one was looking. I spent the rest of my evening pouring cocktails and wondering if she'd still be parked outside when I got off work. She wasn't.

I'd crawled into bed, defeated and a little upset that she couldn't wait on me. Then again, I hadn't asked her to, and it wasn't like we were a thing—yet. I knew I'd have to tell her how I felt sooner or later. She seemed like the type of woman who didn't like to beat around the bush. She was always straightforward with me and everyone I saw her with. I needed to tell her how I felt, but first, I needed to plan an outing together with Maisy and me. I needed to see how Betty would react in certain situations, and then, maybe then, I could feel comfortable enough to tell her without her leaving.

I rubbed my eyes and checked the time on my phone. It was just before dawn—and two minutes before my alarm would buzz. I was supposed to meet Jay for a late morning run. My dad had offered to stay over and watch Maisy so that I could get some time to myself. Lately, since working at The Steamy Clam, I'd not had as much time to work out. Gym time used to be my me time. But juggling two jobs and being a single dad drained me. I missed that endorphin high of a good ass-kicking.

When Jay had asked me to join him on his run, I'd immediately reached out to my dad. He not only agreed before I finished my sentence, but he also told me that I should make it a regular thing.

My morning wood bounced in my gray sweatpants as I rolled out of bed and stretched. I'd purposely dressed in my workout gear because getting up before dawn wasn't my thing. I needed a solid six hours of sleep, and last night, I'd been up well past midnight, tossing and turning and finally rubbing one out to lull myself into dreams of Betty. I shuffled my feet toward my bathroom and readied myself before making coffee and quietly sneaking out the door. The last thing I wanted to do was wake Maisy up. She had fall break this week, and her excitement over the previous days had worn me out.

I drove to Jay and Rox's house, sliding on my shades as the sun made its way up and over the horizon. The coffee I'd poured touched my soul with the first sip, giving me a moan that could rival the moans I'd let Betty strangle out of me.

Betty ...

I rubbed a palm over my tired face. No matter what I did, I couldn't get thoughts of her out of my brain. Betty this and Betty that. She was everywhere. Yesterday, I had seen a poodle with those same tight curls she'd worn weeks ago, and I'd felt a jiggle in my pants. Over a fucking poodle! Not fucking a poodle. A fucking poodle.

Damn it, what is wrong with me?

Love on the brain. That's what.

I wasn't functioning properly, and I couldn't shake the feeling. I wanted to shout it from the rooftops that I loved that woman. But common sense told me to keep my mouth shut.

But what if she wants to tell me she loves me and doesn't? And I don't tell her? Then, we'll both never know, and we'll die as old farts, never knowing we loved each other.

I pulled into Jay's drive and finished my coffee, hoping the caffeine would wake up my dumb brain. My eyes snapped to Betty's house next door. I knew she was an early riser. She had to wake early to prep The Pink Taco Truck.

"She'll be up shortly, mate. Her blinds will open, and then you'll know," Jay said, making his way toward me and opening my door.

"Thanks," I said, hopping out of my truck. "I wondered but figured I'd wake her if I texted. Not sure she would want to see me at the last minute anyway."

"I'd certainly try. See if her blinds are open when we get back. I'm sure she'd love to see you." Jay motioned for me to follow him.

"Really? What makes you say that? Did Rox say anything?" I bounced. I couldn't hide the pep in my step.

"The girls mostly keep their secrets to themselves. But I do know that Betty had a blast with you in Memphis."

We stepped onto a running trail beside Betty's house that led into woods. I'd never been to this park before, but I knew several other runners from Scarlett Herb had recently begun claiming it as their jogging spot after Jay introduced them to it.

If I were a runner, I would have too. The thick canopy of colored leaves almost entirely shielded out the sun. Only filtered light shone through, illuminating a fairy-tale-like forest. I wondered if Betty ever came out here. By the looks of her well-manicured lawn and flowerbeds, I doubted she had time to work out. I'd seen the crap she ate. Tacos, tequila, more tacos, more tequila. She had either been incredibly blessed with good genetics or she worked out in whatever time she could find. I guessed the former. Her family had all looked like they didn't age past thirty.

"You okay back there?" Jay called.

His feet hit the trail in front of me while I lazily followed behind, taking in my surroundings.

"Yeah, yeah. You don't have to wait up. I'm just admiring the beauty."

And thinking of the booty ...

Jay slowed to a stop, letting me catch up. "And?"

"And?" I scraped the bottom of my shoes on the dirt, kicking a pebble to the side of the path.

"And ... what's on your mind? Besides Betty."

"Nothing. Just Betty," I sighed. "Oh, and the fact that I love her and can't tell her yet because before I make that commitment, I need to make sure she's the right fit for Maisy and me. And then she might not love me anyway, so I don't know why my mind is going in circles. And then I'm trying to slow my schedule down at the club. And then—" I droned.

"Stop," he said, holding up his hands. "Did you just say you love her?"

"Yeah." I shrugged my shoulders to my ears before letting them fall, defeated. "I love Betty."

"Congratulations, mate! That's wonderful news!" He clapped me on the back, beaming.

"Is it? She's a lot to handle. And what if she doesn't feel remotely the same way?" I rubbed the back of my neck, which had tensed into a hard knot.

"You have to take risks. I don't think she'll turn you down. I've seen her face light up when she speaks to Rox about you. I think you're good. But you should tell her now. Why wait? We never know what tomorrow might bring." He began walking on the path again, picking up his pace and motioning for me to join him. "Come on."

"But you don't think it's too early? That I might scare her away?" I said between breaths.

"When you love someone, you love someone. You don't choose a time frame. There are no rules. Besides, you two have known each other for a while. You've been friends. Now, you just feel a little something more. And you're not in the friend zone anymore, so I say, go for it."

"Okay. You're right. It's so stupid of me to wait. I'll do it. Maybe when we get back, if she's up." I dug my heels into the ground, pushing myself off faster. Seeing Betty was all the motivation I needed to blow through this early workout.

NINE

Betty

My doorbell rang as soon as I finished the last sip of coffee.

Damn it, Rox. Always running out of creamer.

I tightened my wool robe around me and shuffled my feet across the cold floor. Coming back from the stifling Memphis heat to the cooler mountain air of Outer Forks had been a cruel shock to my system. Before too long, it would begin snowing, and I wasn't cut out for that type of weather. At the first hint of a snowflake, I hibernated.

The doorbell rang again.

"Damn! I'm coming!" I shouted, grabbing the creamer from the fridge and heading toward the front door. "Here, bitch. I bought this one just for you." I opened the door and shoved the creamer in Terrance's face. "Oh!"

"Uh, thanks? I actually take my coffee black, but it's the thought that counts, right?" Terrance grabbed the creamer from my hand.

I snatched it back. "This ain't for you. I thought you were Rox! What are you doing here anyway? Couldn't get enough?" I asked, taking in his white T-shirt and gray sweatpants that perfectly outlined what he was packing down below. I looked to the left and the right, checking for neighbors before reaching out to grab him by the dick and pulling him inside. I couldn't help myself.

"Wow. Okay. Wait. Am I interrupting your shower?"

"No. Why do you think that?"

I threw both of my arms around him and bit his neck. He tasted salty. I remembered Rox mentioning something about Jay and Terrance running one morning.

"Because you're in a shower cap," he said, stepping back and rubbing where I'd sunk my teeth into him.

"This ain't a shower cap! It's a sleeping bonnet." I recoiled back from him like he'd just aged me twenty years.

"Oh. Looks like a shower cap to me." He shrugged.

"And that's why you're getting the punishment. Boy, don't tease me. Don't you know I'll unleash on you?" I reached for my bonnet and threw it across the room, releasing my curls in one big bounce.

"Oh, gosh. Please do," he breathed out, stepping into me. "I need to lie back and let someone else take control for a change. That someone being you."

"Done. You know where we're going. March." I smacked his ass and pointed him to the stairs. I quickly grabbed my phone and followed behind him, sending a text to Rox, saying I'd be thirty minutes late.

> Rox: Jay told me. Have fun. I'll start prepping in the truck. If you hear a commotion in your driveway, it's me.
>
> Me: And if you hear a commotion coming from your old bedroom, it's Terrance.
>
> Rox: Got it.

"Where do you want me?" he asked, looking around at my sex contraptions.

"In the shower. Rinse off. I like my men fresh. Now, go on, through those doors. Towels are under the cabinet." I nodded toward my bathroom door. "Don't take too long. I've got to get to work."

"Okay. Me too."

As soon as he disappeared behind the bathroom door, I ran downstairs into my bedroom. I'd had to get rid of Terrance for a minute, so I could shave my bush and change out of my granny panties I'd slipped on last night. I hadn't expected company, let alone my boy toy standing on my front porch when I wore my wool robe and hair bonnet. I cringed, grabbing a razor and lathering up my bits before shaving myself smooth as quickly as I could.

I heard the faucet turn off upstairs, so I picked up a towel and wiped my taco clean before running back up the stairs and pausing, breathless, as if I'd been standing there, waiting on him the whole time.

He stepped out of the bathroom in a cloud of steam with nothing but one of my starched white towels wrapped around his waist.

"Took you long enough." I smirked. "That's one spanking right there." I tried to hide my heavy breathing.

"Sorry. I wanted to make sure I was fresh." He tilted his head and grinned, dropping the towel. His boyish dimples peeked through a stubbled five o'clock shadow.

Terrance balanced the perfect mixture of pure and edgy. I could barely conceal my excitement over finally coaxing his fine ass back into my dungeon.

I dropped my robe and turned toward my toy shelf, picking up a Fleshlight, a condom, and handcuffs before crawling on top of my bed. I felt his gaze on my back, burning hot as a furnace.

"Come here. To the edge of the bed," I said, patting my comforter.

He nodded, obeying me.

Good boy.

I ran my finger along his chest, down to his cock, and straight up the shaft, watching it flex at my touch. I gripped the head of his dick in my palm, steadying it.

"Let's do some drills." I smiled, spitting on his cock while I looked up for his reaction. His eyes grew wide as I slid his cock into the Fleshlight and eased his hips at an angle. "That's it. Fuck it. Gently. Slow."

He leaned his head back and closed his eyes.

"Nope." I slapped his ass hard. "Watch me while you do it."

He nodded, biting his lip and moving his cock in and out of my toy. His eyes never left mine again.

I watched the way he moved his body, admiring how his abs flexed with each stroke. I wanted to reach out and touch them. I ached to feel that flex under my palm. But I needed to be in control, and I needed him to know he had no power over me. That was my kink, and nothing made me as horny as playing the role of Queen B. Besides, he'd said he wanted me in charge. We were a perfect match.

"You like that?" I asked, grinning.

He nodded back at me.

"Good. Do it to my mouth." I situated myself on the bed, flipping my head toward the edge and hanging off of it.

"Oh fuck," he exhaled.

I opened my mouth and let him ease his dick down my throat. I'd done throat-training before. My gag reflex was nonexistent. I performed this special talent when I wanted to own a man, and I wanted to own Terrance. Ever since the Memphis trip, he'd been on my brain. I'd even deleted all of my dating and hook-up apps. I didn't need them when I had the most satisfying man by the balls already. And if I didn't have Terrance by the balls then, I'd have him now. Literally.

I closed my eyes as his balls brushed up against my lashes. His cock gently fucked my throat while he made the most animalistic moans I'd heard come from a man. I put my hands on his hips and pushed him away so that I could breathe for a second.

"Don't come. Not yet." I pulled him toward my mouth again, making sure he kept watching me.

He groaned, easing himself back down my throat. I spread my legs, inviting him to touch me. He immediately took the hint and reached over, circling my clit before dipping his fingers inside. He worked his cock and fingers faster, plunging them into me so quickly that my knees began to shake. An urge built up inside me, releasing in a sensation I'd never felt before.

I pushed his hips away, sitting up on the bed and looking at my soaked sheets.

"Did you just make me squirt?" My jaw dropped.

I'd tried to teach myself how to squirt for years, but I could never do it. It was like trying to tickle myself. It never worked. I had given in to the fact that my body wasn't capable of performing that trick.

"Mmhmm." He grinned, his eyes still locked with mine.

I could see it in his proud smirk. He had tricks too.

"Fuck," I muttered, wet as ever. "Get on the bed." I tossed my head toward the pillows and shakily stood up.

My legs shook like Jell-O. He had barely touched me, and my body had been ready for climax. If Terrance could make me squirt, I wondered if he could give me multiple orgasms too. That was another thing I'd always wanted to happen to me, but not a single man had gotten me there.

I handcuffed his hands to my bedposts and swung my leg over his head, straddling his face. I wouldn't touch his dick anymore. I wanted him to beg for it. But as much as I tried to hold out myself, I couldn't. I rode his face hard, sliding myself back and forth across his lips. I watched his hips buck up and down. His cock dripped, and as much as I wanted to lean over and take him in my mouth, I let him yearn for it.

I turned myself around so that I could hang on to my headboard. My knees were already shaking enough, but the way Terrance's tongue flicked against my clit had me about to topple over and roll off the bed.

"Mmm, baby. Don't stop." I reached over, remembering I'd had stashed a small whip under a pillow.

I gripped it tightly and swung it behind me, smacking his leg. He groaned, muffled between my thighs, as I hit him again and rode harder. I turned my head, peeking behind me at his hips fucking the air. I cracked the whip against his chest, watching his cock bounce up and down. His wrists strained against the cuffs, popping his biceps out into a flex that had me hanging on to the back of the headboard for dear life.

"Make me come," I said, tilting my hips and grinding against his face.

He moved his head back and forth, licking me in the steady pressure I needed.

Damn, this man knows how to work a woman's body.

I threw the whip across the room and gripped the headboard with both palms, curling my knuckles around them until it hurt. A flush spread from between my legs, throughout my entire body, settling into my cheeks. The bubbly feeling pulsing through my veins shook my whole body in one long, intense wave of pleasure. My throat began to burn as I yelled louder and louder, slowing my pace against his lips.

I heaved myself off him, kissing his lips, slick with my wetness. I barely had the energy to unfasten his cuffs, but the fierce look he gave me told me I'd better do it—and now.

That was what I wanted from him. My goal hadn't only been my pleasure. I craved drawing out that primal desire from men.

"Good boy. Now, fuck me," I commanded, uncuffing his wrists and tossing him the condom.

He wasted no time in slipping it on and slipping it in, growling with a ferocity I'd only heard once in my life. That had been at the zoo when I watched a lion bang his mate.

The sound that wild animal had made was a roar that shook me from the inside out, just as Terrance was doing now. I wrapped my legs around him and curled my fingers over his biceps, steadying myself as he dived into me, rough and with a little pain, just how I liked it.

I felt another urge inside me again. But this time, it wasn't a squirt. This time, it was something in my voice. I needed to get it out. The pain of holding it back was just as bad as the pain of holding back my release earlier. I couldn't help it, and I had no idea what it was until he began to spasm.

His cock throbbed inside me as I pulled him closer, tighter, and screamed out, "Fuck! I love you!"

Things became awkward fast. His pace slowed to an abrupt stop, but he didn't climb off of me. Instead, he held me there, brushing my messy curls from my face.

"I mean ... you know what I mean. Same thing as you did. Endorphins making me dumb. I didn't mean that. Heat of the moment and all." I patted his butt in the friendliest way possible and pushed him off of me. "Wow, look at the time. That wasn't as fast as I'd intended. I'm going to be late!" I ran to the bathroom and shut the door, emptying my bladder, cleaning myself up, and stalling my next move.

"You can't hide in there forever, babe," his voice called out.

"Damn boy using my own words against me," I muttered to myself before plastering on a brave face and greeting him again. "I know; I know. I'm not trying to. I'm—" I began to protest.

"Hey. It's okay," he said, rising from the bed and embracing me. "That was just the passion talking. I get it."

I detected something in his voice.

Sadness? Disappointment? Tiredness?

"I'm going to get rid of this thing," He pointed at the rubber hanging off his dick. He grabbed his clothes and disappeared into the bathroom.

By the time he came back out, I had my robe tied around me again, waiting at the doorway to see him out.

"Thanks for stopping by for some morning delight." I winked, ushering him down the stairs and out the door.

"My pleasure," he sighed. "I was actually stopping by to ask if you'd come over this week. Maisy has fall break, and I thought we could do something fun. She's been asking about you."

He stopped at the front door, turning toward me and squinting as if he was trying to read my thoughts. Thankfully, I had a poker face like no other. There was no way he could tell I was ashamed I'd mumbled those three words that I hadn't even meant.

Did I mean them?

"Sure, sure," I said, opening the door. "Just text me when. I'll have to make arrangements for the truck, but I can afford to take a little time off."

I caught sight of Rox hopping out of the back of the food truck and waved her away. I didn't want to speak to her in front of Terrance. My emotions had already escaped from my mouth enough for this morning.

"I'll let you know. Probably Thursday, if that works." He cupped my chin and leaned down to kiss me.

"Yep. See ya, Tito!" I kissed him back and pushed him out the door, locking it behind him.

I took three steps before collapsing on the floor, and I stared at the ceiling in a state of, *What the fuck just happened?*

The rest of the day dragged on. I worked in silence, not yet ready to confess my mistake to DTF. I didn't feel like hearing Layla's teasing, and Rox would see right through my bullshit anyway. Nikki would probably tell me to stuff a crystal in my twat. I didn't have the energy to think about those three words I'd mumbled. So, instead, I focused on work.

I made tacos quicker than we could sell them, which was saying a lot. Our crowds doubled during the warmer months and showed no signs of stopping even though the weather had been cooling down quickly. I passed the food through the window to customers, lost in my thoughts and not my usual spunky self.

Every time Layla began to question me, Rox would reach out, grabbing her hand and shaking her head.

"Betty will speak when she's ready," she said.

"I just want to make sure she's okay. Nobody died or anything, right?" Layla's eyes were wide with a terror only she could conjure up.

I knew her crazy mind had thought of several different scenarios, which I had to admit, made me feel a little guilty.

"No, no one died." I sighed.

The relief of hearing me utter just those words was satisfying enough to appease her. She nodded, turning back to the food on the stove.

"It's just that—" Layla began.

"Damn it, Layla. You're going to feel Betty's wrath if you keep it up." Nikki stuck her finger in the air and made an X in front of my face, no doubt marking out any negativity I was about to spew.

But for once, I wasn't feeling evil enough to bite.

"It's fine. I just had rough sex this morning, and I'm worn out, is all." I leaned against the countertop.

Our afternoon rush stopped finally, and now was just as good a time as any to lie through my teeth, so my friends would leave me be with my thoughts.

Rox glanced at me from the corner of her eye.

"Well, why didn't you say so?" Layla clapped me on my back. "Happens to me all the time! I did that last week! That was the day I was late. Sorry!" She laughed, turning off the stove.

The parking lot was empty, which meant it was time to move on to our dinner location, near the city's park. Another concert was playing tonight, and we tried not to miss those.

"Who was it this time?" I smirked, turning the subject around on her.

Layla's face grew red. She turned around and stuck her head in the fridge, mumbling, "Oh, just some guy I have on call for when I need that stuff. You know, whatever his face is."

"Whatever his face is. Does this guy go by the name of Aiden?" Nikki blurted what we all suspected.

"No! Gosh. Will y'all give it up? Aiden and I are just friends," Layla huffed, slamming the fridge door shut.

I knew she was full of shit. Terrance and I had been just friends too. And whether I liked it or not, Layla and I had something in common. We were falling for the men we'd placed in our friend zone.

"I'd love to tease you and poke fun at you, but I'm too damn tired. I need some air before we get back to it," I said, opening the back door and hopping out.

"Wait! Me too!" Rox followed behind me and shut the door before anyone else could escape.

We walked down the sidewalk, past the university. A group of girls sat, huddled under a tree, with books piled up around them.

"Could have been us, Rox," I said, tilting my head toward them.

"We were never the college type. Can you imagine us in class? I don't think the teachers could handle us. But then again, those girls look like they're hard to handle too."

We kept walking, watching one of the girls jump up and thrust her hips back and forth in the air while the others laughed.

"Kids these days." I said.

"Yep, kids these days," she echoed.

We walked a little farther before I stopped and turned toward her. She pulled me in for an embrace. She had known this was coming. We'd known each other long enough, and we were always there for one another when needed. I loved DTF, but my connection with Rox was a bond I shared with no one else.

I stepped back from her and shrugged. "He's got a kid."

"Yep."

"And I don't think I'm ready for that kind of responsibility." The words hung in the air, and a weight lifted off me as soon as I said them.

"Why?"

"Why what?"

"Why don't you think you're ready?" she asked, shifting her weight from one foot to the other. "Because you're amazing with your nieces. And you always say you want a family. You aren't getting any younger."

I put my hands up in protest. "Don't start that biological-clock mess."

She gently pushed my arms down to my sides. "Listen to me. You know it's true. Why don't you think you're ready? Why do you keep pushing? You have everything you need. If you wait until you're ready, you'll never get what you want. So what he has a kid? From what you've said, she's amazing. I'm not saying you have to marry him and become her mom. But give Terrance and Maisy both a chance. He can't help that he's a single dad. It's not like you have anything or anyone tying you down. If you can't handle all that comes with dating a dad, then stop. But I know you. I see the way you're falling for this man. It's the same way you were falling for that race car driver you never stopped talking about—the one who got away. Terrance isn't going anywhere that I know of. Do you?"

I shook my head, rubbing my fingertips in circles along my temples.

"See? What's the worst that could happen if you let yourself into a relationship with either of them?"

"I'll get hurt somehow."

"Exactly. A fear every single person has. But you know what's worse than not feeling that vulnerable?"

"Yes. Never knowing," I breathed out, looking behind me and back at the group of girls, still in a fit of laughter under the tree. I started walking back.

"So, you've thought this through already." She hooked her arm in mine.

"I'm so far gone; it's scary as fuck." I shivered.

The wind picked up, blowing leaves in our path.

"I don't know anyone who has the strength you do. And I'm betting you that Terrance is too scared to piss you off. Give it a chance. Who knows? This time next year, you might be pregnant with that family you want!" Her arm tightened against mine as we rubbed hips, walking back toward the food truck.

"Shush!" I laughed, knowing she was right.

I did want a family. I longed for the mother I never had, and since that would never happen, I'd be that mother myself. To my kids, my nieces, Maisy, or any child who came into my life. I'd never let a child feel the way I had, growing up. And I'd do all I could to give them all I hadn't had. Same as Terrance had told me before. We'd both been on the same page in that regard.

My phone chirped in my back pocket.

"Speak of the devil," Rox muttered.

I pulled my phone out and read the text. Sure enough, it was him.

"He wants me to go to some trampoline park and lunch tomorrow. With him and Maisy." I shrugged.

"See? I told you it was him. Divine intervention! Right on time." Rox pressed her fingertips to her lips, kissed them, and threw them toward the sky.

"Here we go again. Yada, yada. You and Nikki and your divine intervention and hocus-pocus," I said while I texted Terrance back that I'd be there.

"You know it's true," she said as I shoved my phone back into my pocket and continued walking.

"Maybe just a little," I admitted.

This last year, things had fallen into place for DTF that I couldn't even explain. It was like all the hard work and effort we had put into our lives and business for years were finally beginning to pay off. The timing couldn't have been any better. The people showing up in our lives weren't anything like the train wrecks we used to tolerate.

"Well? Did you say yes?" She elbowed me, beaming.

I grabbed her hand, turning the back of it toward me and pushing my fingertip into her latest tattoo—a heart melded with golden-yellow seams.

Kintsugi.

"I said yes." I pursed my lips, staring at her.

Rox squealed a Layla squeal that grated my nerves in a way I hadn't known could.

"But if you make that noise again, I'm going to take this divine intervention and shove it up your ass."

"Yes! See? You're still yourself too. You got this, Betty." She gripped my hand, pulling me into her as we stumbled our way back to the truck in a fit of giggles and newfound hope.

TEN

Terrance

Betty had said she loved me, and I didn't have the balls to tell her the truth—that I loved her too. Not just fake, passionate, heat-of-the-moment love. But I truly, truly loved her. I should have followed Jay's advice and manned up, telling her my real feelings. But I wasn't only considering my feelings. I had a little girl whose opinions mattered way more to me than anyone else's. And for her, I'd need to make sure Betty was the right one for both Maisy and me.

"Daddy!" Maisy burst into my bedroom and crawled into bed beside me. "It's your day off! What are we going to do? Can we go see dinosaurs? I heard they were at the zoo. Grandpa said, but I think he might be off his rocker because dinosaurs aren't real anymore. Are they?" Her eyes searched mine, and she had never looked so much like her mother before.

Guilt pierced through my heart for Jane. She was missing out on the best moments in life.

"Off his rocker? Where did you hear that from?"

I put my arm around her and held her tight. It seemed like yesterday when I could cradle her in my hands, and now, she grew taller and taller day by day. I knew she wouldn't let me hold her much longer. I lived for these rare moments when I didn't have to work crazy hours, and I could just be here with my daughter and do the dad thing.

I'd never thought of myself as a dad, but when Jane had found out she was pregnant, I'd become determined to fake it until I made it. Or at least, I was still faking it. I wasn't sure anyone, especially me, ever made it. But my little girl was happy, albeit a bit starved for attention from me. I was working on that as best as I could, but her private school tuition wasn't cheap.

"YouTube! Duh!" Maisy laughed, hopping out of bed. "Come on. Get up! Let's get going!" She patted her palms against the side of the bed as if she were playing the drums.

If there was one thing my daughter didn't lack, it was energy. She woke up energized, she went to bed energized, and when given any form of sugar, she drained my very soul. Which was the exact version of Maisy I needed Betty to see so that I could determine how well she handled my daughter. If she could handle Maisy at her worst, letting Betty into our lives would be a piece of cake. This test would seal the deal on my confession of love—or not.

"Ugh. I'm an old man. I can't just hop out of bed like you." I groaned, rolling off the bed and landing on my feet with a ta-da.

"Okay, boomer!" she said, running off.

I shook my head and made a mental note to limit her iPad time on YouTube.

When I was finally dressed, I made my way to the kitchen, seeing she had already poured us bowls of cereal. Mine had turned into a soggy mess of what looked like sawdust, but I sat down in front of my bowl and ate it anyway.

"Took you long enough! This is my third bowl!" she said, pointing toward her breakfast. "I made you coffee, too, but I think it might be cold now."

"I see," I said, picking up a muddied cup of brown water and sipping it without wincing. "You're quite the lady of the house these days! Thanks, darling." I swallowed my cereal one mushy spoonful at a time.

Maisy had already dressed too. She wore a fuzzy white sweater with a fox print on it—her favorite animal—and a pair of sparkly pink leggings. Thankfully, Maria had done all of the shopping. But now, with her gone and my on-call babysitters starting back up with school, I'd need to take Maisy shopping for her fall wardrobe.

"Hey. I haven't told you this yet, but remember Miss Betty?"

Maisy stopped chewing and slowly nodded her head. Her hair flew out from around her face, framing it in a chaotic mess of curls, much like Betty's. Except Maisy's chaos wasn't intentional. Brushing her hair was like pulling teeth—a dreaded ordeal I had to battle every morning.

"She's going to join us for some fun today. Is that okay with you?" I dipped my head, trying to read her gaze, which had fallen back down to her cereal bowl.

"Because you love her?" she whispered.

"What? No!"

"Do you love her more than me? Does she have kids? Will you love them more? I want a brother or sister. But I'd rather have a puppy." She put her spoon down and took a sip of water, waiting on my response.

"I'll never love anyone more than I do you. You don't ever have to worry about that. No, Miss Betty doesn't have kids. If you aren't comfortable with her coming for our outing, she doesn't have to. You're my number one priority. This day is for you," I said, preparing myself for the fallout of canceling on Betty.

"No way! I want her to come. I like her. She told me to kick boys in the quaffle balls. And guess what. I don't even have to do that! I just have to threaten it!"

I rubbed my palms over my face, shaking out both exhaustion and disbelief.

"Did someone try to bully you again?" The hairs on the back of my neck rose.

I was usually an easygoing man. But one slight to my daughter, and I became daddy bull. Or daddy bear. Whatever was the male equivalent of a dad about to go on an ass-kicking spree.

"No. No one messes with me. This boy at recess kept following me everywhere, so I told him that, and he finally left me alone."

"Maybe he just wanted a friend, Maisy." I squirmed in my seat. The thought of my child becoming the bully terrified me.

"No. He wasn't following me like that. He was following me to annoy me. Making loud animal noises and sticking his tongue out behind my back. I told him he did *not* have my consent to be in my personal space, and if he didn't stop getting too close, I'd kick him in the quaffle balls. That's when he left me alone."

I stuck out my hand for a high five. She slapped her tiny palm against it hard and beamed back at me.

"Proud of you, kiddo. You tell people when they're making you uncomfortable. But let's leave the violence as a last resort. And only if you're defending yourself against an attack, okay? Then, you kick the hell out of his quaffle balls and run!" I hugged her before getting up to put our dishes away.

I'd need to call the school and tell them to watch the students better at recess time. For the price I paid for my daughter to attend there, each child should come with a damn bodyguard.

"So, about this Miss Betty. Is she going to see dinosaurs too then?" she said, tilting her head.

"Dinosaurs at the zoo exhibit—which are fake ones, by the way. Lunch and the trampoline park. And then ice cream and back home." I mopped up the spilled milk on the counter, going over my plan in my head.

Surely, all this fun and excitement would send Maisy into a whirlwind and Betty into a crisis that she would either handle like a badass or fail at miserably and run away—just like Jane.

Maisy squealed, hopping out of her seat and clapping. "I'm ready!"

"No, you're not. Let's brush your hair first. Then, we'll get Miss Betty. But you promise to be on your best behavior today, okay? Miss Betty doesn't have kids. I'm not sure she understands how exhausting it can be, keeping up with you. So, let's be mindful of that." I gently pushed her toward the bathroom, where we'd battle with a hairbrush for twenty minutes.

"Got it. Miss Betty is Daddy's girlfriend," she said, giggling and hopping down the hall in more energy than I'd had all week.

I dragged my feet behind her. My stomach bubbled anxiously. I desperately didn't want to set today up for disaster, but as a single father, I had to know if Betty would fit into my small family or if she was just another runner when the going got tough.

We made it to the zoo before lunch, stopping to pick up Betty along the way. She and Maisy chatted during the entire car ride about everything under the sun. Neither one tired out on conversations. They kept chattering away right up until we exited my truck and made our way through the zoo entrance, and even then, they only stopped talking because the sound of monkeys distracted them long enough to follow their calls.

I'd thought Betty would feel like a third wheel during this outing, but so far, I was the one falling behind. I tried to push myself into the conversation, but these two girls droned on and on without stopping. It became hard for me to get a word in, much less offer an opinion. I tried that during talks of Harry Potter and was immediately shot down. Two against one. I tried to root for Hufflepuff, but these boasting Gryffindors weren't having it.

Maisy walked in the middle of us, grabbing my hand on her left and Betty's on her right and tugging us both toward the monkey exhibit.

"We're going to miss them playing!" she yelled, hurtling us toward the animals.

The closer we came to the monkeys, the louder they *played*. And by *played*, I meant, fucked. We walked up to the exhibit just as Monkey Bobo was pounding Monkey Hoho from behind so loud that Betty and I both winced in pain.

"That's a funny way to play." Maisy looked up at me for answers.

I looked to Betty, horrified.

Not today, Satan.

Today was not the day I explained the birds and the bees to my daughter because we'd stumbled upon two apes going apeshit on each other. Hell no.

"Oh, that is just …" I said as another monkey climbed behind Hoho and began humping her and bellowing at the top of his lungs. "Oh God. What are they teaching these animals?" I cried out to Betty, grabbing Maisy's hand and steering her out of there.

Betty wore an expression as horrified as mine. Clearly, this was territory we both weren't prepared to tackle. I couldn't count this one against her.

"You know, that's a funny way of playing! I don't think that monkey asked for consent to treat others so hurtfully. Looks painful! I wonder if that's a bully monkey, and we're just witnessing a fight. That other monkey should turn around and kick him in the quaffle balls and run. Someone needs to teach that poor animal how to stick up for herself!" Betty grabbed Maisy's other hand and pulled her farther away from the mating calls before turning to me. "Isn't that right?"

"Right. I didn't want you to see a fight and have it scare you. Animals do crazy things sometimes. They aren't people, like us. They're wild. Now, let's go find the mechanical dinosaurs we came here for and grab a bite to eat!" I brushed the top of Maisy's head, calming the look of concern that had furrowed her brow.

Maisy shrugged and skipped ahead.

I sidled next to Betty and put my arm around her waist, pulling her in close enough to hear my whispers. "That was quick thinking. Thanks. I haven't approached that subject with her yet. And I don't plan on it for another forty years."

"No worries. You've got time. Not forty years. Maybe two or three. But she's over it. Look at her. She probably isn't even thinking about wild monkey sex right now. I am though. That one move he did there at the beginning brought back memories of the hotel." Her soft voice tickled my neck, sending goose bumps up my arms.

"You liked that move, didn't ya? I'll have to call it the Bobo now." I laughed.

"Do it, and you'll never do that move on me again." She laughed before returning her gaze to Maisy.

"Don't like that." I shook my head.

"Can you two quit cuddling back there and kick it up a notch?" Maisy turned around, hands on hips.

Betty's mouth formed a small O before she whispered, "*Dayum.*"

We were now entering Maisy's hangry phase, easily recognizable by the lousy adult-sized attitude.

I smiled to myself. *Let the games begin.*

We hustled up beside Maisy as she led the way into the dinosaur exhibit. Her little legs darted from one of the dino robots to the next.

"Do you know what kind of dinosaur this is?" Betty asked Maisy, stopping to read the blurb in front of a severely outdated machine. The robotic figure in front of her hissed. "Puh-lease, robo dino. I got a T. rex next door that could eat you alive." She rolled her eyes.

"I do! It's a dilophosaur."

"How did you know that?" Betty stepped back.

"I can read." Maisy pointed to the blurb. "But what do you mean, you have a T. rex next door?"

Betty threw both her hands in the air. "Oh, okay. It's not a real T. rex. It's one of those costumes my friend likes to wear for shits and giggles. I mean, shoots and giggles! Or whatever." She shot me an apologetic look and shrugged.

"I know what that word means. Sometimes, when I can't find Daddy, I'll go running around the house, screaming for him. He always screams back, 'For goodness' sake, can I please take a shi—' " Her voice became low but loud as she mocked me.

"Whoa, whoa, whoa!" I cut her off, pulling her away from Betty. "Let's get lunch."

Betty smirked and at least averted her eyes from mine to save me some dignity.

"Ice cream?" Maisy's eyes widened.

"No. That's a snack. We need real food." I shook my head and headed toward the exit.

"But I want ice cream. You said we could have ice cream today." Maisy planted her heels in the ground and crossed her arms.

"We can ... but not yet. Let's just get pizza at that restaurant by the elephants. We can watch them while we eat. Sound okay?" I could feel Maisy's hangry attitude growing by the minute.

"No." She stared me down.

"What would you rather eat?"

"Ice cream. Or nothing. Do you want me to starve and die?" She clutched at her chest, falling to her knees and letting out a croak.

"All right, Maisy. We don't have to eat right now. Show me the elephants, will ya? I haven't seen one of those since I was your age. Where to? You're the tour guide for us. Otherwise, I'd get lost in here." Betty stepped in, helping Maisy to her feet.

"I can do that easily. I come here all the time. Or ... I used to. But Daddy works a lot now, so ..." Maisy slumped her shoulders forward and shuffled her feet out of the exhibit and toward the elephants.

"Go on ahead. We're following." Betty nodded, encouraging Maisy onward. "I'm guessing Miss Maisy usually gets what she wants." She turned toward me, hooking her arm in mine.

"Yep. I spoil the shit out of her. She doesn't have a mom or siblings. Hell, we don't even have a pet. And I work all the damn time. Dad guilt. I give her all I can. I do my best. I'm not quite sure how to balance it all. I worry I'll create a monster, spoiling her as I do. But right now, she's just hangry. She gets super moody when that happens. Otherwise, she's as sweet as can be. Usually." I stared down at my shoes, kicking rocks off the path.

"You're her hero. Whether you spoil her or not, you'll figure it out. You just need more help. A village. Also, some tricks, like distraction. That move I pulled back there with telling her to show me the elephants? That was a trick. We're going to go to the elephants and work our way toward the food. Just watch. You have to give her some amount of control too. Kids want that independence. Just like we do. But, hey, you're doing a good job, Terrance. You're a great dad." Betty leaned over, pecking me on the cheek.

Maisy started to bounce in front of us, picking up her pace as she neared the elephants.

"Thanks. I'm trying," I said, jogging to catch up with my daughter before she disappeared out of sight.

"Ta-da! Your wrinkly, old giants await, madam!" Maisy threw her hands out, motioning toward the elephants.

"And what an amazing little tour guide you are! How do you remember where to go?" Betty put her arm around Maisy, bringing her in for a hug.

"Just smart, I guess." Maisy shrugged, leaning on the iron fence and sighing.

We watched the animals eat, walk around, and eat some more, and even though the stench was stifling in this area, my stomach rumbled with a gnawing hunger so loud that it drew Betty's attention.

"This is boring," Maisy said. She gripped the railing and leaned back, bouncing on her heels.

"Yeah, these things are kind of slow. Let's move on. But I need to make a pit stop to the ladies' room first. I think I remember there being one in that restaurant over there." Betty tilted her head toward the place I wanted to sit for lunch. "Want to come with me and wash your hands from the stench of this place?" she asked Maisy.

"I'll show you the way!" Maisy skipped ahead of us again, only pausing to hold the door to the restaurant open for us. "Wow. It smells good in here! Much better than out there!"

"Yeah. It's making me hungry. I might have to get something to eat real quick. After I wash up." Betty ran off to the restroom, followed by Maisy.

When they came back, they both were in a fit of giggles.

"What's so funny?" I asked.

"Girl talk, Dad!" Maisy looked at Betty.

Betty looked back and winked. "Sorry! Girl code. What happens in the ladies' room stays in there. Now, where's that menu? I'm starving!" she said.

"Me too!" Maisy jumped in the air.

I looked at Betty in awe. If Maisy weren't here now, I'd for sure tell her I loved her. She'd been able to not only handle hangry Maisy, but also get her to do something I wanted without bribing her or giving in to her. She manipulated my daughter so flawlessly that I'd propose marriage right here, right now if I could. With Betty's help, this parenting gig was a hell of a lot easier.

We all left the restaurant in much better moods. I ordered Maisy an extra-sugary ice cream sundae to eat in the truck on the way to the trampoline park. Maisy plus sugar plus a giant gymnasium full of kids screaming and hollering would be the ultimate test. If Betty could handle that, she was golden. I could barely even handle that combo.

I reached over to hold Betty's hand as Maisy ate her ice cream and sang at the top of her lungs. Lately, she'd been into the band Queen. I'd been playing their top tracks on repeat for weeks. It could be worse. It could be that damn "Baby Shark" shit I kept hearing everywhere.

"You've got one cool kid there, Terrance. Listen to her. Singing Queen, knowing her dinosaurs. I bet she can show me some warrior moves at this trampoline park too," Betty said loud enough for Maisy to hear.

"I can beat Daddy at the ropes course," Maisy said, smacking her lips.

"It's true though." I nodded.

"I bet. Are you sure your arm is okay to be playing at the trampoline park?" Betty asked, turning in her seat.

"Of course. I don't even have a cast anymore. It's like a new arm! Look!" Maisy jerked her arm back and forth.

"It's fine. I asked the doctor. Everything is all good," I assured Betty and myself.

We pulled into the parking lot, hopped out, and bought our tickets. I insisted Betty jump with us, and she didn't argue. But once we walked past the entrance and into the gymnasium, she began to change her mind.

"What's that?" She pointed at a kid flying down a zip line.

He screamed at the top of his lungs, swaying side to side until he came to an abrupt stop on the other side of the gym.

"That's the zip line! I've been trying to get Maisy to do it for forever, but she's too chicken." I stuck my palms under my pits and performed a chicken flap.

"Nuh-uh! I'll do it. I just might not do it today. That's all!" Maisy jumped up and down, pulling us toward a giant trampoline.

"I don't blame you, Maisy. I don't think I'd do that either. I'm not a fan of heights!" Betty glanced at the ropes course, also high up on the ceiling.

"But you flew in an airplane!" I said.

"That was different! I wasn't hanging there, like that kid!" She tilted her head toward a little girl who was screaming in terror as she hurled toward the end of the zip line. Her legs were kicking out from under her while her parents watched from below, snapping pictures on their phones.

"Let's jump. The highest person to bounce gets more ice cream!" Maisy bounced on the trampoline.

I gripped Betty's hand and led her onto it before starting to bounce slowly. She watched my moves and tried to mimic me, failing miserably. Instead of bouncing, she looked like she was squatting to pee.

"Do you—" I was about to ask her if she had any clue as to what she was doing before she cut me off.

"Black people don't do this shit," she whispered, snapping her eyes to mine. Then, she smiled and waved at Maisy, who had bounced across the entire trampoline and back.

"Yeah, they do! I think it's just Betty that doesn't do it. Bend your knees slightly! Like this!" I paused, going over the motions on how to jump on a trampoline properly.

"I got it. I got it." Betty bent down low before leaping into the air. She landed hard, bending her knees and bouncing back up higher and higher.

I'd never seen someone jump so high. The way she wobbled when she was in the air told me that it hadn't been intentional. Her eyes grew wider, the higher she rose.

"How do I stop? Make it stop!" she yelled.

Maisy fell over in a fit of giggles. Even I grabbed myself. Otherwise, I'd piss my pants.

I could barely breathe from laughing so hard. "Stop bouncing!"

"I can't! My legs won't bend. They'll break. Help! Help! Get that man over there," she said, pointing to a worker.

"You don't need that man. Just stop! Put your legs out. Land on your butt!" I screamed at her, hoping she could hear me way up there.

Whatever magic juju she used to fly to the top of the damn gym looked like something straight out of a movie. Even I became terrified for her. But that didn't stop Maisy or me from laughing. By now, a small crowd had gathered, watching in awe as Betty screamed with each bounce.

"To hell, land on my butt!" she cried.

Maisy put her hand over her mouth. "She said a bad word!"

"Trust me," I shouted. "Throw your legs out. It won't hurt! That's all you can do unless you want to bend your knees and slow it down."

"Move outta the way!" she snapped, throwing her legs out from under her and crashing down on that juicy booty that I knew would soften her landing. Kind of. She bounced left. She bounced right. She somersaulted to the side and landed facedown and ass up.

I clenched my jaw, my fists, and my butt. Betty was going to kill me for this.

I ran to her side. "Are you okay?" I said, picking her up.

She brushed herself off and shot me a look that shut me up real quick.

"That's the end of that. You owe me." She pursed her lips together and looked to Maisy, paying me no more attention. "What else is here? Anything less dangerous?"

"The Q-tip battles!" Maisy shouted. "You and Daddy do it!"

"What's that?" Betty asked as Maisy pulled her toward the battlegrounds.

"You get these giant Q-tips, and you knock the other person off the ledge. You fall into foam. It won't hurt. I get Daddy all the time. Don't worry. He's easy!"

We rounded the corner to what I liked to call the war zone. The giant room hummed with inflatable obstacle courses—whirling inflatable games to knock you off your feet, ropes you had to swing on or fall into the foam pit of death, and the Q-tip game where you were allowed to beat your opponent with a giant bar.

"Oh, I gotcha. I used to watch them do something like this on TV when I was little." Betty smirked before leaning over to whisper in my ear, "Since you wanted to laugh at me back there on the trampoline, do you know what I'm going to do now? I'm going to whoop your ass with this Q-tip. And after that, I'm going to pick you up out of that pit and whoop it again."

I nodded, biting my lip to keep from laughing. It was all I could do. I had known after that stunt with the trampoline, I was due for punishment. I'd only hoped that punishment was in her sex dungeon and not here on the battlefield among all these innocent children. I looked left and right at the kids whooping each other's asses at their stations. No one would even notice my poor self being pummeled by this demon spawn I'd brought to the children's park.

Maisy sat on the side of the pit, giggling, as Betty walked the plank toward me, armed with the giant Q-tip across her chest. I tiptoed toward her, wondering if I should just jump off and surrender. I glanced down at the pit below me for half a second before I felt a wallop to my right shoulder, knocking me into a tumble off the plank. I looked up, dazed and unsure of what had just happened. Betty stepped into my view, blocking out the light like the devil coming to take my soul.

"Round one," she sneered.

"Ooh, Daddy. You're losing!" Maisy yelled, bringing my attention back to her. "You can do it! Get up!"

I climbed out of the pit and reluctantly started over again, inching my way down the plank and toward the wild woman. I noticed her hair was messed up. If I told her that, she would knock me clear across the damn room. Better that I kept my mouth shut. I straightened my back, holding the Q-tip out in front of me, blocking her from that ninja move she'd pulled earlier. It was like she had come out of nowhere.

"Someone is stalling again. You like doing that, don't you?" Betty shouted down the plank.

"What was that again? I can't hear you. Maybe you should get back on the trampoline. Clear your mind with fresh air up there," I said, pointing toward the ceiling.

Betty's nostrils flared as she barreled toward me. I held my weapon out at arm's length. There was no way she could get through me. I smirked at her, but then she swiped her giant Q-tip clear across my legs, knocking me off of my feet and back into the pit.

"What's that? Forget to bend your knees and jump? How do you like it when your legs fly out from under you and you land on your ass?" she called down to me, grinning.

I groaned. "I surrender. Can we do an obstacle course or something less painful?"

I looked at Maisy to save me. She peered over the side of the pit, wide-eyed, nodding.

"Thanks, peanut," I croaked out.

Betty put her Q-tip up and walked to me, shaking my hand.

"See? Good sportsmanship. Always be friendly to your opponent." She smiled at Maisy.

"You really whooped his ass, Miss Betty!" She bobbed her tiny head up and down.

"Maisy! You can't use that language!" I said, cringing and looking around to make sure no one else had heard my parenting fail.

"It's true though," Maisy said, hopping along to the next stop.

We followed her into the obstacle course, dodging inflatables, climbing ropes, and flying down slides. Maisy begged us to go through it all again eight times before she became bored enough to move on to the next contraption. Betty's hair lay plastered to her head. A bead of sweat rolled down her brow before she reached up and wiped it away, fanning herself.

"How does your child have this energy?" she huffed, watching Maisy bounce up and down, pulling at my hand to keep going.

"Siphons it out of me," I moaned, mopping sweat from my brow too.

"I want to do the zip line." Maisy paused in her bounce, staring at me. Her face had gone white.

"What? Really? Why?" I asked, leaning in to make sure I'd heard her right.

"If Miss Betty goes first." Maisy looked up at Betty with her big puppy-dog blue eyes that got me every time.

I doubted they would work on Betty. I doubted anything would work on Betty. Especially after the trampoline stunt.

"Child, you got a thing or two to learn about me." Betty shook her head.

"I have learned. You are pretty. You are brave. You are strong. You kick bullies in the quaffle balls if they hurt you. And my dad likes you. I do too. I'll do it if you do it." Maisy curled her hand around Betty's palm.

Like the grinch, Betty's heart grew so much that it nearly burst out of her chest.

"Let's go." She sniffled, clutching Maisy's tiny hand.

They shuffled their feet toward the zip line in total silence. Neither one of them made a peep, which was incredibly out of character for both of them. I hadn't heard either one of them be quiet for more than a minute during this entire outing. Or actually, ever.

"It's going to be fine. Want me to do it first?" I stooped to Maisy, who stood below the zip line, watching kids hurtle down the track.

"No. What if you get hurt? I don't want you to. It's too dangerous!" she protested, pushing me back toward a chair. "Sit and watch Miss Betty and me. Girl power, right, Miss Betty?"

Betty looked like she was about to be sick. "Girl power!" She threw a limp fist in the air before marching off to face her fears.

"Proud of you, kiddo! You got this! You too, big kiddo!" I called out.

Betty turned, narrowing her eyes at me and making the motion of cracking a whip above my head. My cock began to thicken so quickly that I had to cross my legs and put my hands in my lap so as not to look like a perv in the trampoline park. Betty had me out of my element, and I had her out of hers. My plan had come along nicely, and she had aced the test. After this, I'd be done with all the games. She'd already won.

I craned my neck up toward the jump-off of the zip line, watching both my daughter and Betty strap themselves into their harnesses. Betty checked Maisy's straps not once, but three times. I nodded in satisfaction. Maisy peered over the edge before backing up and shaking her head. Betty leaned down, whispering something and flexing her muscles. She kissed Maisy on the forehead, turned toward her death sentence, took a deep breath, and jumped.

I'd never before in my life heard the noise she made. Down the track came screams of what I could only describe as the howls of a wraith, a demon, or a siren. Whatever monster crawled from the depths of hell to feast on your soul, that was the sound Betty made. After this stunt, I would be in for the worst punishment of my life.

Everyone stopped in their tracks to watch Betty hurtling toward the other side of the gymnasium. Their nervous eyes glanced toward me in knowing sympathy.

Take pity on me. I've been a bad boy.

I had reached the point of delirious fright. I had been so damn terrified during this whole ordeal that I burst into laughter the second she flew by me. I gave a halfhearted wave as she passed by, slicing through my soul with her evil-eyed stare. Her hair flew out behind her like a black death veil. She held her body stiff as a mannequin. Nothing moved on her, except her eyes and mouth. I winced, watching her hit the exit with a thud. I quickly looked up, catching Maisy's eye. There was no way she would jump off the zip line after watching that spectacle.

Maisy turned to me with a look of horror. She tiptoed toward the ledge, peering down and pouting.

I yelled up at her, "You don't have to do it!"

She shook her head, straightened her back, and looked straight ahead. "Right in the quaffle balls!" she screamed, jumping off the edge and hurtling down the track in the exact same howl and stiff body she'd seen Betty perform.

I watched her disappear toward the back, screaming until I heard the thud and silence again.

I ran to the other side of the gymnasium, eager to make sure both of them were okay. I caught them as they shakily made their way down the stairs.

"You're so brave!" I shouted at Maisy. "How did that feel? You were amazing! Don't you feel great now?" I squatted down, hugging her before holding her at arm's length.

She took one look at me, flashed green in an instant, and hurled all over my shirt.

ELEVEN

Betty

After my outing with Maisy and Terrance, I had come home and crashed. Even working The Pink Taco Truck and going to The Steamy Clam on my late nights didn't tire me out as Maisy had. The poor girl could run her mouth and her little body nonstop. I'd been babysitting my nieces since their birth, and even they didn't wear me out like Terrance's daughter had.

The next morning, I sat at my dining table, sipping coffee and scrolling through the latest headlines. Nikki had warned me to stay away from the news. There was nothing good about it. Very rarely would I stumble across a positive, uplifting story. If I needed that, I'd have to make one myself. I did my best to add some of that good juju to the world. I didn't carry around crystals as Nikki did or volunteer at the shelter like Rox. Instead, I focused on being the best person I could be to the people who passed through my life.

Case in point, Maisy. As tiring as that little girl was, I tried my best to show her the female that she would need to be to make it in this harsh world. I wasn't the type that bullied anyone to *toughen them up*. I'd hated it when my aunts and uncles did that to me. Life was tough enough already. To toughen anyone up, they only needed to be taught. I already had it all figured out. I'd raise my kids the same.

Whenever I have kids …

My mind drifted to my biological clock. I wasn't too old for children yet. But I'd need to know a man for at least a year before I married. And then I'd need to be married for a year before I started trying for a kid. My eyes rolled up to the ceiling as I calculated the math in my head.

Shit. I need to get started.

I'd been asking myself for a while now, *What exactly am I waiting on?*

I had a good man in front of me. Yes, he was a package deal, but I happened to like that package deal. Maisy seemed like a good kid. She only needed a bit more guidance from a female figure. Her dad could try to help her out when she hit those teenage years, but I couldn't see Terrance having a sit-down meeting about a menstrual cycle. And the only talk he would have about boys would be him threatening to kill them if they touched her.

I shook the thoughts out of my head.

What am I thinking?

I'd barely been awake an hour, and already, I was planning my life with Terrance. Me. Betty. The one who was wild and crazy and never settled down. I didn't know why or how Maisy and Terrance felt right with me, but they did. I could do this. I wanted to do this. I didn't want to grow old and miserable like my mother, changing men with every season. I wanted a family. I'd always known that. Terrance and Maisy weren't what I'd had in mind, but nothing ever worked out the way we thought it should.

I picked up my phone, ready to dial Nikki and discuss fate. Maybe I needed to open myself up a bit more, and if I did, I needed her super-positive outlook and crystal-loving vibes to help me with this. I could play the part of badass

Betty, but yesterday, that little girl had stolen my heart. That was some scary shit.

I thumbed through my Contacts list, searching for Nikki's name, but a text from Terrance came through, interrupting my mission.

> *Terrance: You are so amazing. Maisy can't stop talking about you, and she wants to know when you'll be back.*

I smiled at the phone, feeling those damn butterflies again. I preferred to think of them as little electric shocks, like from a shock collar—something to wake me up and warn me before I became too dumb. I grinned at the idea of a shock collar. My dungeon needed new toys.

> *Me: She's super sweet. I'm glad she had a good time, except for her getting sick. She bounced back quickly though!*

> *Terrance: She always does. Nothing gets her down.*

> *Me: I see that. Is she staying with your dad today while you work?*

> *Terrance: Yep. I'm on a mission to find another babysitter or two. Steady ones this time. He needs a break just as much as I do. Someone told me it takes a village, so I'm searching for my village.*

> *Me: You can use me if you'd like sometime.*

> *Terrance: Oh, I'd love to use you. In more ways than one. Speaking of, I was wondering if I could stop by after my shift. I know you work late, but if our times match up, I'd love to stop by for just a quick chat.*

Me: Chat? Why do you have to bullshit? You know you're ready for this ish.

I untied my robe and took a quick photo of my breasts before sending it to him.

Terrance: Damn. You are so damn sexy. Like a midnight sun.

Me: Midnight sun? What is even a midnight sun?

Terrance: I don't know. I was trying to be all romantic and sexy with words. Woo you. I should have just said you're beautiful.

Me: Let's go back to Queen B. But, yeah, I should be done by 10-10:30 tonight.

Terrance: Okay. I'll do my best to head out of the restaurant by then. I'll let you know if I'm running late. I know I can get Jay or Aiden to cover for me though.

Me: You think they're going to let you off early, so you can fuck your girl?

Terrance: Something like that.

Me: I'll see you here tonight then.

I set my phone down and patted my hair. Our outing had royally screwed up my hairdo, but it had all been worth it. I permitted myself to feel everything and not cram it down into the pit of my stomach like I usually did. Hell, I was so head over heels that I even considered letting Terrance play boss in my dungeon for the night.

Work had passed by quickly, as usual. Both of our taco trucks could barely keep up with the workload, and with Earl pushing us to open a standing restaurant, we began to consider it.

"We don't need another truck or another restaurant. Earl is just itching to reinvest. You know how he likes to keep rolling that money out. If we had a stand-alone restaurant, our truck sales would drop. And I know y'all don't want to stay in one place. The open air does us all good." Rox swung a dish towel over her shoulder.

"I'm just saying, it's getting to be a bit much. Something has to take the pressure off. I'm not able to do as much these days because of the youth center." Nikki sighed.

"And I'm still working the shelter on my off shifts." Rox threw her hands in the air.

"I don't have anything to do! I mean, I do. I have been taking dance lessons with Aiden. It's our new hobby. But I can chip in more or help figure out how to grow or whatever you need," Layla said, dancing around the tiny truck kitchen.

"So, you admit, you and Aiden are more than friends now?" I raised my brows.

"What? No! I just always wanted to learn to salsa, and he offered to go too. Said he needed to get out of the house and do more than hit the bars. We've only been twice, but it's fun. Y'all should go. Just saying." Layla untied her apron and hung it on the hook.

"I've got time. A lot of time. But Earl isn't going to let up until we expand. I just don't know how that could happen. I'll get with Layla this week, and we can get some ideas going and run it past you two." I nodded toward Rox and Nikki.

"Really?" Layla's jaw dropped open. "You want to meet with me? Who is this creature, and what did you do with my beloved, foul-mouthed Betty?" She made the sign of the cross.

"Keep teasing, and she'll put a foot in your ass, reminding you just who you're talking to," I clapped back. "Besides, I'm turning over a new leaf. Trying to embrace positive energy and change my attitude a bit."

My besties dropped what they had been doing and stared at me. I'd quietly contemplated how to tell them and ask them for their help. I'd never had a serious relationship, and with Terrance, I wanted to give it a shot. I didn't want to run him off. Sure, I'd had my heart broken before, but I'd never let myself open up enough to give back love or even accept it. The whole concept of mushy feelings was foreign bullshit to me. But I'd watched Rox and Jay, and I'd seen Weston and Nikki, and whether Layla wanted to admit her love for Aiden, I'd seen that too. They were all beginning something I wanted, and I would soon be left behind—the single old lady.

"I knew it!" Layla smacked her palm on the edge of the counter before pulling it back and wincing. "You're in love!"

Rox's eyes locked on mine. "Proud of you, babe. So, you've decided to take on the dad and kid after all?"

I had yet to tell any of them about my outing with Maisy and Terrance. Sometimes, instead of talking out my issues like a normal, stable person, I'd sit on them and think. I'd tell myself that, eventually, I would open up for advice, but usually, I never did. Instead, I kept that all inside. But new Betty spilled the beans. I told them about the pervy monkeys, the trampoline fiasco, the ice-cream incident, and the way I felt about all of it, which was … different. Warm, fuzzy, and not myself. But in a good way.

By the time I finished telling them, Layla had ruined her mascara from crying, Rox was beaming with her golden smile, and Nikki was clutching her crystal, whispering something that sounded like a protective spell.

"So, now, he wants to meet for a quickie after work." I crossed my arms, ending my story.

"Why the hell are you still here then?" Layla threw her arms in the air. "Go! Love him!"

"Yeah, why are you still here?" Nikki eyed me.

"Stalling. Classic Betty. Not new Betty. Stop stalling. Go fuck your man. Y-O-U-R man. Because, you know, you got him now. It sounds to me like you're both in this, and you need to have that conversation tonight to see that you're on the same page. If not, one of you will get hurt." Rox tipped her chin at me. "That would be you."

"Don't ruin the rose-colored glasses she's wearing! Let her feel all of it! Even if it might hurt." Layla shrugged her shoulders and avoided my gaze.

"Why are you two saying I might get hurt? Do you know something I don't?" I glanced at all three of them, sticking my hip out for emphasis, preparing myself for a boob drop.

"Take this. It's black tourmaline. We only want to protect you." Nikki pulled a pouch out from her back pocket, fished around for a tiny pebble, and pushed it into my palm.

"Black tourmaline? Are you giving me a black crystal because I'm Black? Black-girl magic? Is this because I'm dating a White man?" My body stiffened.

"Well, we can all agree that the old Betty is still in there. And she'd damn well better be. Black tourmaline is for protection, you twit. It also acts as a positive force for good in your life. We all want the best for you."

"And if that doesn't work, you got a voodoo doll I can have too, right?" I tossed my hair and performed the boob drop.

"Of course," Nikki said. Her eyes sparkled.

"And I know a man." Layla snapped her fingers in the air, bobbing her head.

"And I'm screwing his boss, so ..." Rox crossed her arms.

"DTF," I sighed as they pulled me in for a group hug.

"DTF!" they murmured back.

I washed up when I arrived home, texting Terrance that I would be ready a little late. I needed ample time to get myself together. And by *get myself together*, I meant, I needed to make sure I shaved my chocha, prepped my dungeon, and calmed my nerves with a cocktail of my own making. I had no idea what I was doing, mixing drinks, but I went with it. I named my new cocktail the Black Tourmaline. It was much like an old-fashioned with a twist of blackberry instead of orange.

I rolled the crystal pebble around in my hand before stuffing it into a tiny pouch that clipped into my bra. I wasn't one to dabble in hocus-pocus, but for Terrance and this hot, melty feeling, I'd try. I made two drinks and set the record player on a smooth jazz record handed down to me by my aunt May.

I propped my feet up on the coffee table, leaning back and sipping my cocktail, thinking of how Aunt May was right. She had seen this coming from a mile away. Who could resist Terrance and his chiseled, scruffy jaw or his rock-hard six-pack abs or his sweet-ass dance moves? The way he gyrated those hips on the dance floor was the same way he moved them in bed. He gave me a pounding that even I wasn't used to—and I had done some wild shit.

I heard the knock on my door and threw back my drink, finishing it faster than I would have liked, but they didn't call it liquid courage for nothing. I sauntered over toward the door in my sexiest sashay before realizing I looked dumb as hell and needed to check myself. I needed to be myself—or at least new Betty with a mixture of the old Betty. Not this cuddly teddy bear I was quickly becoming. That was dangerous. I had to have boundaries. I was still me even if I felt all the things, like this new beginning I was embarking on. I turned the knob on the front door and took a deep breath.

I got this ish.

I did not have this ish.

"Hey you!" My voice came out about eight decibels too high.

"Hey …" Terrance tilted his head, probably gauging how much I'd had to drink.

"Come in. Sit. I made a special cocktail." I sauntered over to the wet bar beside the record player. Some jazz singer I didn't know droned on and on in a soft, sultry voice.

"Oh? Tell me about it." He followed me to the record player, putting his arms around my waist and leaning into my neck. He brushed my hair to the side, planting a kiss at the nape of my neck before breathing me in one long, deep inhale.

That was when things became fuzzy.

"It's strong. Like me," I breathed out the words, standing there like an idiot, holding his drink, but not turning back around. I didn't want to. I wanted to stand here forever and let him smooch on my neck some more. It curled my toes, gave me those damn butterflies, and soaked my panties. I wanted him to make me his. This was so not me. I blamed the black tourmaline.

He reached around me, taking the drink from my hand and turning my body to his. He took a slow sip, wetting his lips and closing his eyes. "Mmm."

He leaned down, brushing his mouth against mine. The alcohol tingled against my lips.

I breathed into his mouth, closing my eyes and swaying. Surely, this was the alcohol making me goofy as hell. Not this feelings shit.

He set his drink back down, took my hand in his, and danced with me. His arms circled my waist, arching my back until I met his gaze while he swung his hips with mine, clutching me tight enough that I felt his cock thicken against me. The jazz artist sang louder, my heart beat faster, and my brain left the building.

So, this is love, I thought, letting myself fall.

"You're incredible. So damn amazing. You check all the boxes. You passed the test." He leaned down, kissing my forehead.

I thought I'd heard him right, but I wasn't quite sure.

"What was that?" I looked up at him, pulling my brows together in what I hoped looked innocently curious. Instead, my tipsy ass probably looked like I was fighting back an ass-whooping. Which, in hindsight, I was. My body subconsciously knew it—or at least the black tourmaline crystal did.

"I said, you passed all the test. You're amazing." He kissed my forehead again.

"Hold up." I stopped dancing, pushing him away so that I could look at his face. "What do you mean, test?"

His eyes darted around the room, avoiding mine. The jazz singer droned on and on, but this time, her song no longer sounded sultry. She sounded mad. I felt my ears burn hot.

"I mean that I wanted to make sure you could handle Maisy. And me. I needed to know so that I could move on. With you!"

He reached for my shoulder, but I dodged him with those ninja moves I'd learned during his *test*.

"You're telling me, you set me up?"

"Well, that's not the right way to put it. I didn't set you up. I just wanted to make sure, for Maisy's sake and mine, that you were the right one. And you were. Are. I …" He backed up, running his hand through his hair. His face had turned white, and his shoulders sank into his chest.

He cowered, and I grew taller. My nostrils flared, my back straightened, and I pulled myself up to my full height.

Nope, that wasn't love. Nope. False alarm.

"You set me up. You purposely tried to give me a rough time to see how I would react with your child. What, you didn't trust me? Didn't think to ask me? Couldn't you have just voiced your concerns like a normal human being? It's because I told her to kick that kid in the nuts, isn't it?"

"No. Not at all. Besides, you said quaffle balls! That ... that's not it." His voice came out sounding like I'd kicked him in the quaffle balls, and by some small miracle, I hadn't.

Maybe he had a black tourmaline tucked in his drawers too.

"Then, what is it?"

"I had to make sure you were right."

"You mean, good enough?" I walked over to the record player and turned it off. I picked up his drink and drank it all in one big gulp. "Because that's what it sounds like to me. You wanted to send me through some asshole game, a test, throwing all sorts of obstacles against me to check if I was good enough. You couldn't just talk to me about your concerns and let me spend time with Maisy. Normal time with her. You did all that craziness on purpose? Hyping her up with sugar, the trampolines, showing me all her energy— you did that on purpose." I set the glass back down and walked to the front door, opening it.

"I guess I did. I didn't see it that way. Shit. I'm sorry." He rubbed the back of his neck.

"I think you need to go. I don't know who you think I am, but I'm not one to play games. I also don't tolerate bullshit. I thought, by now, you knew that. But it looks like you've got a lot to learn from your Queen B. She doesn't bow to anyone like that. You almost got me." I bit my lip hard, fighting back the tears that I'd sworn I'd never let anyone see. Not even Rox had seen me cry. "You almost fucking got me."

"I'm such an idiot. I fucked up so bad," he mumbled, walking through the doorway and pausing.

"Yep," I said, shutting the door in his face.

I couldn't look at him any longer, or he'd see just what he had done to me. Instead, I crumbled to the floor and waited until I heard him pull out of my driveway. When he left, I let myself cry.

TWELVE

Terrance

I drove home with my tail between my legs. One moment, I had been on cloud nine, preparing to tell Betty I loved her, and the next, she had kicked me in the quaffle balls. I'd never thought of my test as an asshole move until I'd actually stopped to think about it. She was right. That was dickish of me. And for me to make her feel like she wasn't enough was the ultimate blow for her. I knew that from listening to her talk about her past.

I groaned, gripping my steering wheel until my knuckles turned white. I'd fucked up big time. I'd ruined something that I'd not felt in forever. Not since Jane had left anyway. I was terrified of losing Betty—or even worse, of Maisy losing Betty. And my dumbass had pushed her away. I'd sent her packing with my stupid game.

I made it home with my brain on autopilot. Maisy and my dad were both fast asleep on the couch. A child's movie was playing in the background.

The next few nights, I'd have to work at the club. But I had planned on asking Jay for another day off while Maisy was on break. I wanted to spend one-on-one quality time with her without all the sugar and mischief.

I missed her during my long shifts, but the money was flowing in, and soon enough, I'd have a regularly scheduled job with better working hours. With Jay's talk of expansion, if I couldn't open my own bar, maybe I could take command of the new restaurant. Either way, I needed more time with my daughter. And now, with me having to break the news of Betty possibly not seeing her again, she would really need me.

I leaned down, scooping her off the couch and cradling her like I had all those years ago when she was just a baby in my hands.

"She's so grown, yet she's not, isn't she?" my dad whispered, sitting up on the couch.

"Still my baby," I whispered back, holding Maisy tight while subconsciously rocking her like I had on those long nights when she was a newborn.

"And she will be walking down the aisle before too long too. Right when you blink." He smiled.

"Shh! Don't say that!" I said, looking down at my sleeping beauty and realizing she would one day be a grown woman and move away.

"That's why you need to cherish these moments. And make more of them. Also, she needs to see what a healthy relationship looks like. How's Betty?" He pulled a cover on top of him and sat back.

"I know; I know. I'm going to request another day off this week. Sit down and get my shit together. I'll have a little more time on my hands. Betty let me go."

Maisy stirred at my voice.

"Let me put her in bed. I'll be right back," I whispered to my dad, tiptoeing up the stairs and tucking Maisy into bed.

She let out a little snore, rolled over, and fell back asleep. I flipped on a night-light and stood in the doorway for a minute, watching her. I could be a stripper or a mixologist or a royal fuckup, but nothing defined me more than being a dad. For Maisy, I'd do anything.

I dragged myself back down the stairs, preparing for an attack. I'd finally found a good woman, and I'd ruined it. My dad would no doubt let me know the test had been a dumb idea.

"You can't tell Maisy," he blurted as soon as I rounded the corner.

"What? Why? I'm going to have to tell her sometime. I won't tell her details, but I'll have to let her know we won't be seeing Miss Betty." I plopped myself on the other side of the couch and stared back at my future self.

People had always told my dad and me that we looked alike. It was a sad coincidence that the mother of our children had abandoned us. And if I kept up my bullshit, I'd forever be alone, just like him.

My dad leaned forward, grabbing a stack of papers with a card on top, and tossed the card at me.

"What's this?" I opened it up, pulling out a thank-you card, handwritten by Maisy in her favorite color crayon—yellow, for sunshine.

"She made it for Betty. She talked nonstop about Betty. Betty this and Betty that. She wanted to thank her for teaching her to be brave on the zip line," he said.

I opened the card up, noticing the quaffle balls drawn inside along with hearts, a dog, and three stick figures—me, Maisy, and Betty.

"Crap," I said, stuffing the card back in the envelope.

"Yeah. So, don't tell her. At least, don't tell her yet. It'll break that little girl's heart. Besides, what did you do to run Betty off like that?"

I sighed, fidgeted with the card, and told my dad the whole story of my dumbass test. His eyebrows shot up, and his head nodded. He winced and cringed a few times, but he never said a word. He only rose from his spot on the couch and came over, patting my head like I was ten. Then, he told me to get some sleep.

"That's it? No fatherly advice?" I asked, confused.

Surely, the man who had been urging me to find a woman for both myself and Maisy would have something constructive to add to my predicament.

"I don't need to offer you any advice. You know what to do already. And if you don't have the quaffle balls to do it yourself, do it for Maisy. Course, you need to let Betty cool down for a few days. But that's it. No longer. Don't let her think she doesn't mean anything."

"She does. I love her." My voice shook.

It was well past midnight, but I was too upset to be tired. I wouldn't be able to rest until I explained myself to Betty.

"I know. That's why you're going to get her back."

"But how?"

"You'll figure it out. Just don't wait too long. A beautiful woman like her will get snatched up fast!" My dad shuffled his feet out of the room and went to bed.

I stayed, curled up on the couch, contemplating my next move until I finally ended up dozing off into a restless slumber.

The next few days flew by in a blur. I'd worked for Scarlett Herb and finished a few shifts at The Steamy Clam, but losing Betty had brought my entire life into a significant reevaluation. All I ever did was work. Sure, I saved money for *one day*. But I wasn't living in the moment. And even though I didn't run away like Jane, I still missed out on moments with Maisy that I'd never get back. Not to mention, I'd lost myself. I spent my life as a mixologist and a stripper. That was it. I didn't even know who Terrance was anymore.

If I had time to myself and time with Maisy, I'd feel a little more balanced, and I could slow down and make rational decisions. Instead, I made dumb ones, like setting up someone to fail at a test. Betty hadn't failed at anything. If I was honest with myself, I'd tried to make her lose the game. If she had failed, I would have been able to move on like normal with life—not risking anything. But she'd passed, and, well, that was new and scary territory for me.

But I loved Betty, and Maisy loved Betty. Which meant I had a lot of ass-kissing to do.

The next night, I worked my last gig at The Steamy Clam. I apologized for leaving in such a rush, but I had to do it for myself and Maisy. I also consulted with Jay, who agreed to let me go a little earlier on some nights when he or Aiden would take over the bar for me. They were both childless but accommodating when it came to Maisy. I didn't know why I'd kept her a secret in the first place. It seemed that everyone wanted to help me out.

"It takes a village," I remembered Betty saying.

And my village had been here in Outer Forks the entire time. I'd only wanted to be a badass and pretend I could do it all on my own—with my dad's help, of course. But my poor dad was getting older and feeling the strain too. And I hadn't been fair to him. Even though he'd give me the shirt off his back, I needed to get my shit together. I couldn't lean on him forever.

"So, you're only just going to talk to her? No buying her apology jewelry or getting on your knees, begging, or surprising her with a trip to Hawaii? You think it will work if you just speak with her?" my dad asked.

"Yep," I lied. "Betty isn't the type of person who cares about all of that fluff and stuff. She needs up-front honesty. Answers. She needs answers." I ran my hand through my messy hair. I'd already begun shaking.

"What is this? Are we getting a dog?" Maisy ran into the kitchen, a collar and leash in hand.

When I'd told my dad that I wouldn't be buying apology jewelry, I hadn't exactly lied. I'd bought apology sex toys. The leash and collar were for me.

Maisy swung the heavy chain leash above her head in a helicopter move while jumping up and down, shouting out dog names, "Fido! Fifi! Ralph!"

My dad eyed me up and down as I plucked the leash from my daughter's fingers.

"Nope. It's for ... someone at work. Sorry, honey. Gift for a new puppy." I rolled the chain up in my hands and stuffed it in my jacket.

"Big dog. Almost human-sized." My dad grinned, leaning in to whisper, "What the heck kind of kinky shit are young people into these days?"

"Ahh ... uh ..." I cleared my throat and clapped him on the back. "You should get out more. That's all I'm saying. And now that I quit my side hustle, you'll have time. Because this little peanut will be with me."

I picked Maisy up and twirled her around the kitchen. She threw her arms around me and held on tight.

Already, I felt like a weight had lifted off of me.

When I told Maisy that I'd soon be spending more time at home, she lit up like it was Christmastime.

"Can we do something with Miss Betty again too?" she asked.

"Working on it." I kissed her forehead.

And I had been working on it. I'd racked my brain, talked to DTF, and even looked up Aunt May's number and given her a call. Everyone had told me the same thing. Just freaking talk to Betty. Why I had been delaying it, I didn't know. Wait. That was bullshit. I knew. I was scared. And who the hell wouldn't be scared of Queen B? She'd threatened to turn my boss into an alligator handbag. She had a dungeon full of torture devices. She looked like a goddess rising out of the pits of hell when she became riled up, and I loved her for it. Everything about her, I loved it. Her.

I patted Maisy's thank-you card in my back pocket for backup. Either the leash or the card would have to work. Maybe both. I'd still not decided what I was going to do first. All I knew was that I needed to be a big boy and use my words. I'd tell her I loved her, and she would likely bite my head off and save the rest of me for breakfast.

I checked the time on my phone a dozen times before I left. I had no clue what time she would be home, but I would wait on her anyway. I'd sit in her driveway all damn night if I had to.

What if she pulls up with another man in her car?

What if she runs me over when she sees me?

My mind began to race. I knew I was only trying to talk myself out of heading over to her place. But if there was one thing Betty respected, it was quaffle balls. And I was going to show her I had the biggest damn quaffle balls she'd ever seen even if I had to fake it.

THIRTEEN

Betty

I hadn't slept in the days following my breakup. Just when things had been coming together and I had opened my dumbass heart up, Terrance had pulled some stupid shit. Like I was some type of horse and he was a carrot on a stick. Like he'd thought he could throw me into bullshit and watch me fight my way out. I wanted to send him through a round of spankings he'd never forget. But Maisy, poor Maisy, I guessed I'd never see her again.

The following days after his fuckup, Rox had agreed that we wouldn't park our taco truck near Scarlett Herb. I needed to cool down, and running into Terrance while he worked wasn't going to get me there.

I'd told DTF the entire story the day after it happened.

"A fucking game, Rox. That grown-ass man was playing games," I growled, setting my spatula down hard on the counter. Bits of beef splattered against the stove, my hands, the window.

"You're giving him too much credit. He's still a man." Nikki rolled her eyes. "Weston does dumb shit all the time."

"Jay has made several dumb mistakes too. But then again, I have too. We all do." Rox shrugged, wiping up the mess I'd made.

"You're not going to want to hear this," Layla said.

I snapped my eyes to hers.

"But"—her voice shook—"unpopular opinion ... I think it was endearing. He loves his daughter so much that he did whatever it took to protect her. I mean, maybe he went about it in the dumbest possible way. Yes, he could have talked to you about his concerns instead of doing the test. But, again, we are talking about a man here. Their brains don't function like ours." She loosened her apron strings and groaned, rubbing at her lower back and avoiding my evil eye.

"I think you two should talk. He can explain himself, and you can explain how he made you feel. Kiss. Make up. That's what you're supposed to do in a relationship," Rox said.

"But he hasn't called or anything. I've not heard a word from him. Besides, who said we were in a relationship? We never had that talk either." I threw a dishrag over my shoulder and opened the window.

The lunch line was already forming.

"Just don't write him and Maisy off yet. Let everything settle down. You wanted him to trust you and to feel like you were good enough for him without tests or bullshit. He wanted to make sure you wouldn't flee him and his daughter, like his ex had. Both of y'all weren't communicating. Instead, you were keeping everything to yourselves and inventing obstacles. Didn't you take him through an obstacle when you brought him to your aunt May's? If you'd both just talked, no one would have needed obstacles, and everything would have been fine. And I'm guessing you never told him you were in love with him because if you had, I doubt he would have done all that crap. If you two would communicate ..." Layla's voice hit a high pitch that I'd never heard before. She also made sense, and that was new for her too.

I cut my eyes to Rox's, wondering if she'd told everyone I'd fallen in love with Terrance. Rox shook her head.

I paused, taking our first order before jumping back at Layla. "How do you know I'm in love with him?"

"Because we can all see it in your face. Just like our faces that have transformed this year. Rox, me, even Layla—though she won't *admit it either—you … we're all glowing. It's not these damn rocks doing it. It's these damn men." Nikki dragged her fingertips across the row of crystals hanging from the ceiling.*

"And"—Rox sighed—"none of us have really known healthy relationships. We're all trying. This year has been a learning experience. You're learning, just as we are. And I bet the men are too."

I took a deep breath and continued working in silence. I thought about how Terrance must have felt when his mom had left him and how he must have felt when Maisy's mom had left them both. There was no excuse for a grown man to do dumb shit. But fear could make someone do crazy things. And if a stupid test was all his peanut brain could come up with for me, then I guessed it could have been worse. He could have outright lied to my face about something or tested me with another woman.

But still, I had my boundaries, and I wouldn't be the first to say shit. Same with the damn love thing. I would let men come to me. If I meant enough to someone, they'd let me know. I wasn't about to chase a man. Queen B bowed to no one.

After a particularly hellish day in the taco truck, I was looking forward to nothing more than crawling into my bed tonight.

We'd parked at the corporate park today for a change in scene, and dealing with old businessmen was the least favorite part of my job. You'd think those rich, old farts would tip well, but most didn't. They were too busy on their phones to even offer up a thank-you. But we were still avoiding anywhere near Scarlett Herb, and the university was out for fall break. So, the corporate park had our business, and we had theirs.

I'd stuffed so many tacos today for grumpy executives that I was in no mood to deal with any more shit. So, when I pulled the rumbling taco truck into my driveway and saw Terrance leaning against his truck, the fleeting thought of ramming into him flashed briefly through my mind.

Rox must have sensed it because she reached out and touched my shoulder. "Good luck. Let me know how it goes. And, hey, don't forget. We fuck up too. We as in us women. You know it. I know it. Keep an open mind. Don't shut down again. I like this new Betty. Keep the attitude though. Just don't go bitter. Love you." She leaned in, kissing my cheek before hopping out of the truck. She gave Terrance a little wave and ran off to her house next door.

I took my time in climbing out of my truck, partly because I had no idea what I was going to say to him and partly because I was trying to cool down and listen to Rox's advice for once.

I slammed the truck door.

Nope. That's not starting off right.

I paused, taking a deep breath and closing my eyes.

New Betty. New Betty. New Betty. Don't be bitter. Keep the attitude. I fuck up too.

"You okay?" Terrance popped up behind me, causing me to jump and shout for mercy. "I'm so sorry! I didn't mean to scare you." His pale face turned a shade lighter, almost glowing in the dark. He wrung his hands.

The poor man was terrified—as damn well he should be.

Nice Betty. Sweet Betty. Little ball of fur? Be a kind Betty and purr, purr, purr.

"I'm okay." I gritted my teeth, holding back the verbal assault I wanted to give him, but I knew if I opened my mouth, I'd probably end up crying.

"Can you talk? Do you have a minute? I'm sorry I didn't text you first. I was afraid you'd say no. So, I guess I've given you no choice. Fuck. That sounds terrible, saying it out loud.

Shit." He rubbed his palms over his face and stared at the sky.

It was a full moon tonight. I wondered if Nikki would warn against having a serious conversation under this celestial juju.

"It's fine. We all screw up," I muttered, folding my arms across my chest and waiting on his move.

"I mean, I wanted to see you. I needed to see you. Of course, you have a choice. You can go inside, if you'd like. I'll leave. But I hope you hear me out."

"No. You're here now. Say your piece. I'll say mine. Let's hear it. It must have been important for you to skip out on your gig tonight."

"There aren't any more gigs at The Steamy Clam. I quit. Reevaluating my time and priorities." He stepped slightly closer to me, looking scared that I might open my jaw wide and devour him. I might.

"No more Tito?" I asked, taken aback. I'd expected an apology, not a life change.

"No more Tito. Guess you'll have to find another male dancer's drawers to stuff money down." He grinned.

I had to curl my fists to keep my fingers from reaching up and sliding over those lips of his.

"Or I could do better things with my money," I said, not missing a beat.

"That would be a smart decision. I could learn from you. Sometimes, I don't make smart decisions." His voice trembled.

I almost felt sorry for him. Almost.

"You don't say." I pursed my lips, mentally picturing myself putting on my big-girl panties, and let him speak.

"Betty, I'm sorry. I fucked up. Somewhere in my pea brain, I thought that if I put you through that dumb test, you could handle us. You wouldn't leave like Jane. You'd stay for Maisy and me. I set you up. I admit it. You passed with flying colors, if it makes a difference." He unfolded a piece of paper and handed it to me.

I took it, and the chalky writing in yellow crayon smudged my fingertips. Unless Terrance's juvenile ass liked to color, this was from Maisy. I opened the card, read the thank-you, and bit my tongue at the quaffle balls. My heart fell into the pit of my stomach. That little girl was much smarter than her daddy. It wasn't only her who needed the guidance of a woman in her life. It was also Terrance.

"She misses you. I miss you. I'm an idiot. But I learn. I don't make the same mistake twice. Which brings me to something else I need to tell you."

I braced myself. My nostrils flared, my spine straightened, and I threw my shoulders back. He was going to tell me Jane was back. Or he was leaving. Or he had someone else. Or whatever the worst thing my brain could come up with because that was how it worked. That was how it always worked. And that was why there was no gentle, sweet Betty who bowed down and became vulnerable.

"Here goes." He wobbled, putting his hand out and steadying himself against my taco truck. "I knew I loved you that day at Central Station when I told you. It wasn't just me talking shit in the heat of the moment. That was the truth. I love you, Betty," he blurted, taking a deep, heaving breath. He straightened himself up to his full height and stared down at me. "You are all woman, and believe it or not, I can handle you. I want to be that man who can handle you. I want you as mine. All mine."

I turned, pinning my back against the truck. I needed to steady myself, too, preparing for my comfortable chaos, ready to attack. Not to hear those three words, ripe with enough fuel to burn us both up.

"That was hard for me to say. Jeez. I don't know why. It just was. I've been meaning to tell you for forever, but I was just a chickenshit. I didn't want to freak you out and scare you away. Have you ever told anyone that? That you loved them?" he asked, catching his breath.

"No." I shook my head. "I'm also a chickenshit, I guess."

He nodded his head and turned his attention back up to the moon, avoiding my gaze when he asked me his next question, "Has anyone ever told you that?"

"No." My heart pounded in my chest. "Not like this."

"Well, here I am, telling you. I love you, Betty. You don't have to say anything back. I just want you to know that. I know love makes people do stupid things. I'm not excusing myself for setting you up on that damn test. But maybe I'm trying to soften the blow. It won't happen again. I can't promise that I won't be a dumbass again. But I can promise that you'll get open communication with me and that you can trust me."

New Betty. New Betty. New Betty.

Fuck it. I could follow in the footsteps of my mama, cycling through men. Or I could choose to live a bitter life until I became old and senile like my aunt May. Or maybe, just maybe, I could grow some Betty balls and give this relationship thing a try.

"Terrance," I breathed out, "I love you too. I mean, I think it's love. Pretty sure it is. But I don't know how to love a man. I've never seen a healthy relationship. The way I was raised has made me cautious of men. Or not to trust them at least. I never let myself get close." I blocked out ferocious Betty and let myself say whatever came to mind. "But with you … you're different. You're making me feel these things. I'm not sure how I feel about that either. I don't like to feel things that could get me hurt."

"What things?" He stepped into me, reaching for both of my hands.

"A bubbling in my soul. It rises and flutters around in there. My chest tightens, and I catch my breath when I think of you. I want to be with you—always. Growing old and experiencing life. All I do is think of you, all day and every damn day. You're stuck in my brain, dancing around in there with your Tito drawers and making me constantly hot and ready. Like a damn pizza." I shocked myself with my sudden poetic inspiration.

Rox would be proud. I wanted to file whatever ick feelings I'd just put out into the world in my memory bank for her next poetry book.

"Are you comparing yourself to a pizza? Because you know that's the way to my heart, right? Pizza." He pulled me in for a hug, rubbing my shoulders.

"No, I didn't know that. And see?" I buried myself in the nape of his neck, mumbling and too afraid to look into his eyes when I said what was coming next, "It's little things like that, that I want to know. I want to know everything. I want to see everything and do everything—with you. But not only you, Terrance. I want to with Maisy too. And, Lord have mercy, I'm just going to say this shit. I want to have your babies. I want to make a chocolate-and-vanilla swirl. That's batshit crazy, isn't it? I'd do anything for you. Anything. And that scares the shit out of me."

"Betty?" He pulled back.

I couldn't meet his gaze. No way could I look him in the eyes after admitting whatever my dumbass biological clock had made me say. This new Betty was unpredictable, reckless, dangerous, and dumb.

"What?" I said, covering my face with my palms.

"I want that too." He pried my fingers from my cheeks and tilted my chin up. "I'm truly sorry for that dumbass test. I never meant to make you feel like you weren't enough or anything like that. You're enough. More than enough. You're everything."

And those words meant more than the three words he'd said before. I threw my arms around him, partly because I didn't want him to see my eyes tearing up and partly because I needed him to catch me.

"Terrance?" I wiped at my eyes.

"Yes?"

"If you ever trick me again or pull some bullshit, I'll string you up by your quaffle balls and parade you around town as a warning to others."

New Betty but still old Betty, I told myself, satisfied with the balance I'd found.

"I'd expect nothing less of you. I'm yours." He reached in his jacket pocket, pulling a leash and collar out.

I took it from his hand, fastening the collar around my neck and looping the chain through the buckle.

"It was supposed to be for me, but I think I might like this better." He slipped a finger under the leather collar and tugged, biting his lip.

"I know. We can take turns though. New Betty. Your Betty."

I dangled the chain in front of his face. He grasped it, rolling it up around his wrist until he pulled my lips to his and growled. I let myself go, breathing out with the old and in with the new. Besides, if he fucked up again, this chain would double as the most painful whip I owned.

EPILOGUE

Terrance

I pulled my mobile mixologist truck, The Juice Caboose—named after my girlfriend's hot ass—behind The Pink Taco Truck. On weekends, during the winter weather, we'd collaborate on our menus. DTF would churn out churros for my spiked Mexican hot cocoa. Or they'd pair a braised Shizzle Sauce brisket with a hot Shizzle Sauce toddy of my making. Business had grown for both of us, even during the slow season.

When Betty had mentioned to The Pink Taco Truck's founder, Earl, my idea for a mobile bar, he had jumped on the chance to crown me his latest investment—after Betty made him put me through tests to deem my worthiness. Payback was a bitch. I ran a race, learned to knit, volunteered with DTF, found out what those metal balls were for on her sex shelf, and met her mom.

That last test was brutal. I dodged trap after trap with Betty's mom, but nothing she threw at me stuck. Finally, she had accepted me and realized that I was not only good enough for her daughter, but that her daughter was good enough too.

They still didn't speak much, but Betty and her mom would never have the type of relationship she needed. Instead, Betty funneled that energy into being the mother she wanted to be to Maisy. Their relationship had blossomed.

I peered outside of my order window, watching both Betty and Maisy coloring in a notebook. The sun shone warm enough to heat the midday, and the lull that followed our lunch rush was more than welcome. I had thought setting my own hours and being a boss would be great. But I hadn't realized how great. I was still as busy as ever, but I had my girls with me now—both of them. And my dad even worked, helping me out. Who would have thought that bartending also ran in the family?

"I could use a hotty toddy, Tito man!" Betty shouted, glancing at me from behind her shoulder.

"What's the magic word?" I called back.

"Expecto a cocktail!" Maisy said, waving her crayon in the air like it was a wand.

"Nope. Try again," I yelled back.

Betty rose from her chair and marched around the back of my truck, letting herself in and stepping between my dad and me.

"I'm going to leave you two alone for a minute and go help Maisy with her book." He nodded, getting out of Betty's way.

"The magic word, you say? Or the safe word?" Betty pushed me against the counter, leaning in and biting my lower lip.

"Safe word," I moaned. "I'll make anything you want, just keep doing that."

Her fingers fumbled down my abs and went straight in for the kill, grabbing my cock with that familiar strangle move she liked to do.

"Beavis," she whispered before bursting into a fit of laughter.

"I told you we couldn't pick a funny safe word. It ruins the whole moment. Can't we say something like *harder*?" I smirked.

"Lighten up, my man." She elbowed me in the side. "I've got enough coming for you tonight. I am prepping for our honeymoon. I've got to work on my stamina. Talk about marathon sex. Just wait until we get to that exotic place you said you're taking me to."

I tucked my fingers in between her belt loops and tugged her toward me, pushing my rock-hard cock up against her. "Miss Willis, I can't imagine the honeymoon sex you have planned. I'm betting it's not going to be a sweet and clean lovemaking session. But something I can remember. I'm betting you and your friends are planning an entire wedding that is going to be … way outside of normal. Am I right?"

"Of course mine is. Nikki is going the traditional route since they already eloped, and Ma won't get off her ass about having a *real* wedding. Rox is a mix of in between. But you know me; I can't have white cake and pink flowers."

"Why don't you three just have an entire DTF wedding? One big party?"

"What about Layla? We can't just leave her out. She was supposed to be the first one to get married anyway. None of the rest of us ever expected it to happen to us, especially like this."

"What do you mean, like this?" I rubbed my scruffy jawline, where Betty reached up, stroking me softly. Yes, Betty was soft. Sometimes.

"Just so fast. One minute, we were all trying to figure out life, and the next, things just fell into place like they were meant to, I guess. I can't explain it." She stepped aside, leaning against the counter and watching Maisy.

DTF had taken a break, and they were all sitting at a table, passing coloring pages around between them.

"It's like your DTF family keeps growing. But with men. And a little girl. And who knows what next year will bring? Maybe babies." I stood behind her, wrapping my arms around that tiny waist of hers.

I did not doubt in my mind that, in a year, her taut belly would begin growing. We'd both hinted around at wanting children as soon as we were married.

"It's true though," she said, intertwining her hands with mine and tugging me tighter around her.

"And you're okay with your little girl gang growing? All of this happening, as you said, so fast?" I stroked her flawless hair, sinking my nose in her scalp and breathing in her familiar coconut scent.

I didn't need an exotic vacation when I had Betty. She was my escape.

"When you know, you know. Look at them out there. They're all happy. Even single Layla. How could I not be okay with life right now? It's perfect."

She bit her bottom lip hard, sucking it in between her teeth and taking a deep breath. Over the last few months, I'd come to know, that was the way she held back tears. Sad tears, happy tears, painful tears.

We both stood silently, watching Layla dance with Maisy while Rox and Nikki had their heads together, concentrating on coloring a picture. My dad was busy stuffing his face with tacos and laughing with Earl. Even the cold winds couldn't keep everyone apart for long.

"I'd better make her come in and warm up for a little bit at least. She's going to catch a cold out there." Betty nodded toward Maisy.

"You're already an amazing mom. So caring, so sweet, so—"

"Did you just call me sweet?" She shook her head before kissing me with a sharp peck on the lips and climbing back out of my truck.

"Sweet like poison. Alcohol. Shizzle Sauce. Dark and … juicy?" I called out.

"Just stop while you're ahead. You know we still haven't gotten our dirty talk down. Let's add that to the list of things to work on for our great escape. In the meantime …" She blew me a kiss and motioned her arm in the air as if she were cracking a whip.

I winked, letting her believe she was a badass. But she and I both knew that she really had grown sweet.

The more time she spent with Maisy and me, the bigger her heart grew. She even said the L-word to us in front of her friends and family. And me? I didn't need any tests or games to find her worthy. She'd always been worthy.

She was Queen B, and I was her Tito. She had me by the quaffle balls, and I loved every second of it.

PLAYLIST

Do you want to turn up the girl power? Check out a few of these songs from the official *Whip It Out* playlist. For the full playlist, visit Spotify and search for Kat Addams and keep on rocking.

"Black Betty" | Ram Jam

"Won't Bite" | Doja Cat

"Anaconda" | Nicki Minaj

"Nasty Gal" | Betty Davis

"Game Is My Middle Name" | Betty Davis

"Let's Stay Together" | Tina Turner

"I Need a Freak" | Nemesis

ACKNOWLEDGMENTS

As always, for my daughter. May we all raise strong women. Everything I do is for you. That will never change. If a man ever breaks your heart, Mama will kick him in the quaffle balls for you.

Thank you to my diversity editor, Renita McKinney, who helped me look at things from a different perspective. I appreciate everything you taught me. A huge thank you to my editor, Jovana Shirley, who always makes my books sparkle. My books would probably read like a twelve-year-old wrote them without her. Also, thank you to my cover designer, Lori Jackson. I don't trust anyone else with my covers! She is ridiculously talented! Same to my publicist, Kelley Hawthorne. She has given me a wealth of knowledge and guidance in this industry. And last but not least in my business world, thank you to my assistant, Kari Hogan. I couldn't get nearly as much done without you. I have the best team, and without all of these ladies, I would be lost. They are all true DTF.

I owe a lot of thanks to my friend, TE. You are my Betty. Thank you so much for helping me navigate life's crazy curveballs, all while making me laugh. You are a blessing.

Also, thank you to DN for sticking by me when my inner Betty comes out and taking me on anyway. You were put in the right place at the right time, and I couldn't be more thankful. I appreciate your support. All of it.

Thank you to the DTF gang, the bookstagrammers, my ARC team, and all of the people out there sharing and supporting these crazy books of mine. You make me look good! I appreciate all of you and your hard work.

DTF!!!

ABOUT THE AUTHOR

Kat Addams is a forever twenty-nine-year-old fashionista following her lifelong dream of writing contemporary romance inspired by the exotic men she meets in her worldly travels. At least, that's what she would like for you to think. She's certainly not a stay-at-home mom indulging in excessive daydreaming, frozen pizzas, an unhealthy addiction to purchasing pajamas, and one too many cocktails on the regular. That's some other romance author. The poor thing probably has to sneak away upstairs to write her dirty stories! What would her family think? Thankfully, that's not Kat!

Social Media:

Still crazy about Kat? Rawr! Stalk her on the social media platforms linked below!

> https://linktr.ee/author_kat_addams
>
> (For all of the links in one convenient location!)
>
> Newsletter: https://kataddams.com/free-book
>
> (Bonus *Hotty Toddy* Free E-Book)

Want to keep up with all the mischief and bad decisions? Be sure to subscribe to Kat's newsletter for the latest news. By becoming a subscriber, you'll be the first to know the juicy details on upcoming releases! You'll also be the first to hear of special offers, exclusive content, sneak peeks, terrible ideas, ridiculous shenanigans, and more! As a special gift for signing up, you'll also receive a free e-book, *Hotty Toddy*. Check below for more information on this stand-alone, second chance, and fake marriage novella.

> Goodreads:
> www.goodreads.com/author/show/19253462.Kat_Addams
>
> Bookbub:
> www.bookbub.com/profile/kat-addams
>
> Amazon:
> http://amazon.com/author/kataddams

DTF, Dirty. Tough. Females. (A Kat Addams Reader Group): https://www.facebook.com/groups/DirtyToughFemales/

(A Facebook group to stay connected, laugh, and share. Hope to see you there!)

Facebook: www.facebook.com/KatAddamsAuthor

Instagram: www.instagram.com/authorkataddams

Twitter: https://twitter.com/KatAddamsAuthor

ARC Team: https://docs.google.com/forms/u/2/d/e/1FAIpQLScinoImFEIChW3PQ4_BrlBoYxpcClYTftNZRz-1DmI-121R8A/viewform?usp=send_form

(Interested in receiving Kat Addams's latest books before release? Click the link to join the ARC team!)

OTHER BOOKS BY KAT ADDAMS

DIRTY SOUTH SERIES

Hotty Toddy (Free for newsletter subscribers:
https://kataddams.com/free-book*)*

Grit and Grind

Nashvegas Nights

Mr. Big Ego

Mayday

DTF (DIRTY. TOUGH. FEMALE.) SERIES

On the Rox

Cream-Pied

Whip It Out

Just the Tip

Made in the USA
Monee, IL
07 January 2021